PATRIOT TRAITOR

The Augustus Peña Series

Part 2

I0556197

PATRIOT TRAITOR

By O. Nicholas Cicero

ISBN-13: 978-0-9912534-3-2

Copyright 2020 Third Street Creations

For questions and comments about the quality of this book, please contact the author at Cicero-Author@Outlook.com

"I have never shied away from controversy, nor has controversy ever hesitated from appearing at my doorstep."
~ O. Nicholas Cicero

To my beautiful son Alex: I miss you, and I am so sorry.

To my adorable son Julian: You are a precious gift.

To my angelic Aurora: You are my savior, and I love you dearly.

To my daughter Aetna: You are a force of nature.

To my daughter Catalina: Welcome

To Rachel: *Sempare Amore.*

PROLOGUE

In The Augustus Peña Series opener, Assassin's Breach, Augustus killed in the name of family, as opposed to country, after his former director targeted him for assassination as retribution for Augustus having sought permission to write fictional books that bore a resemblance to Augustus' true experiences.

As he engages in battles to save his life, and the lives of his family, Augustus comes into possession of a jackpot lottery ticket worth millions of dollars.

Now, in a strange sequence of events, Augustus learns that he can use this unclaimed lottery ticket to expose the bloodthirsty nature of this nation's top clandestine organization. However, his violent quest to reveal the truth has consequences; with those who support Augustus seeing him as a Patriot, as opposed to those who will kill at all costs to prevent the truth from coming to light, seeing Augustus as a Traitor.

ONE

"Hating people is like burning down your own house to get rid of a rat." - Harry Emerson Fosdick

DES MOINES, IOWA
DECEMBER 2010

Reminiscent of the events leading to this moment, the Des Moines, Iowa weather took a drastic turn for the worse. A blistering wind, combined with blowing snow, made for a hellacious trek to the landing zone for exfiltration. The pickup point was the city's waterworks parade grounds.

C. Virgil Milken, the Director of National Intelligence Covert Operations, referred to as NICO, arrived at the landing zone. However, the chopper was not there. Milken kept walking, both to keep warm and to avoid attracting attention by remaining idle.

Milken pondered how it was that he got to this very moment. He knew that ordering the assassination of Augustus Peña, the darkest and most proficient asset ever to serve within NICO's ranks, carried a certain level of risk.

"That is why I hired Ajax to complete this sensitive task," Milken grumbled. "He was a magnificent talent; the offspring of a legacy KGB family that had gloriously earned Russia's admiration."

Milken assessed the chaos he created. "The task of killing Augustus should have occurred with minimal hindrance. I knew there would be risks, but how could I have anticipated that Augustus' wife would kill Ajax? That was an unforeseen scenario. The fault lies squarely with Ajax. I did not order the murder of Augustus' wife, and two-year-old son. That was a tactical decision Ajax made without seeking, or receiving, my guidance. I do not accept responsibility for an assassin's rogue actions."

Milken stopped walking to glance at his watch. He inhaled deeply, and said, "NICO lost the initiative the moment Augustus' wife blew Ajax's brains onto the roadway. Playing catchup to end this debacle has been a bloody nightmare."

Milken reflected on the carnage incurred by this mission. "The wife killed Ajax, and Augustus went berserk, killing everyone I threw at him. He killed Kjas Brüder, one of NICO's most senior assassins, whom I dispatched to backup Ajax, as a matter of protocol. Not long after, Augustus slaughters the two NSA agents I sent after we lost contact with Kjas. These are immeasurable losses. However, Augustus' execution of the Corsican, and the massacre he laid upon the mercenary team from Belize I sent to finish him off, as well as his family, and those who were protecting them, was catastrophic. This operation has experienced nothing but butchery, and failure."

ॐॐॐ

Milken was not concerned with the pilot's ability to locate him. Years ago, Milken was marked with a tattoo that consisted of ink traceable via satellite, and GPS technology. It was simply a matter of time.

Several more cold and grueling minutes passed in the howling Iowa tempest.

Without warning, the storm's wind patterns changed dramatically.

A menacing squall dropped Milken to his knees. Particles of ice and snow beat violently upon his face, as he attempted to shield his eyes from the onslaught.

My chariot has arrived, thought Milken.

The helicopter landed swiftly. The side door slid open. Milken rose from his knees, and climbed inside.

"Welcome aboard, sir," greeted the pilot.

"What the hell kept you?" growled Milken. The craft lifted as he spoke.

"It has been a busy day for my unit sir, that's for sure," replied the pilot.

"I don't give two shits how busy you are. This is a time-sensitive matter, as are all our operations. That is a pathetic attempt to hide from your incompetence."

The pilot did not retort. He dared not say a word. Emergency Service Corps, referred to as E.S.C., pilots knew that Milken flew choppers during the Vietnam War. They were also keenly aware of his brutal reputation. The greatest fear amongst E.S.C. pilots was of Milken not thinking twice about killing them, and taking over the controls.

Milken calmed down, and said, "I suppose the rapid change in weather didn't help."

The pilot cautiously replied. "The weather had nothing to do with it. There are multiple exfiltration requests from this region."

Milken sat forward, and positioned himself just inches behind the pilot's head.

The pilot experienced a rush of dread come over him upon feeling Milken exhale on his neck.

"What other exfiltration requests do you speak of? I am the only NICO asset out here," growled Milken.

"Not NICO," replied the pilot, shakily.

"Educate me," said Milken, slowly.

"Sir, I have no details about who the exfiltration was for. All I know is that an emergency request came in to support a special operation."

"Where?" asked Milken.

"Omaha, Nebraska."

"Are you going there now?"

"No," replied the pilot. "That is what caused the delay. We were unprepared for two separate recoveries from this region. It caught us off guard. A second pilot is currently headed there."

Milken slowly sat back in his seat. The two men remained silent. Only the chopper's humming filled the air.

Milken thought for a few moments, and said, "Take me there."

"Sir?"

"Omaha, take me there at once!" Milken demanded.

"Sir, please do not do this to me," the pilot pleaded. "There are specific protocols in place that govern these missions. The Omaha removal is for someone not within your organization. I am forbidden from revealing their identity to you, and vice versa."

"I don't give a goddamn about your protocols," shouted Milken, "you take me there now or I will−"

"Kill me?" queried the pilot, anticipating Milken's next words.

"Yes," Milken bluntly replied.

"Then do what you must, sir. I will put this bird down in the open field ahead. Kill me, and fly yourself to Omaha."

Milken stared incredulously at the pilot.

"I am not taking you to Omaha, or anywhere else for that matter. I am an emergency services recovery pilot, not a chauffeur." The pilot proceeded to descend the craft's altitude.

"No, don't do that," said Milken, "continue on course."

The pilot did not respond. He levelled off the helicopter's trajectory, and maintained his assigned course.

Milken stared out the chopper's window. He was perplexed about what other operation in this region would require emergency services.

"It was definitely not NICO," he muttered. He then thought, *domestic agencies, enforcement or otherwise, do not utilize these services. They are not even aware of its existence.*

Milken inhaled deeply, believing he figured it out, and exhaled, saying, "XM."

Shifting further into the darkness of the chopper's interior, he pondered it some more.

Frenchy is dead, he thought, referring to Mauricio di Pecha, the Corsican XM operative that Augustus killed in Des Moines, Iowa just hours earlier. *Prior to Augustus killing him, Frenchy failed to maintain contact with me as I instructed him to do. He must have been orchestrating an exfiltration with XM headquarters in Belize.*

The situation became even clearer to Milken. Although XM had no official status with the United States government, the shadowy entity provided direct critical support to the nation's clandestine services. Consequently, XM enjoyed certain privileges while operating within the United States, to include emergency services exfiltration.

Milken spoke under his breath. "The question now becomes, who are they extracting? The Corsican baboon is dead. It has to be Augustus."

He asked the pilot for his satellite phone. "I need to make an emergency call."

The pilot complied.

Milken placed a call to Prentiss Gates, NICO's second in command, to explain what he learned.

ຈ∕ຈ∕ຈ

"**W**hy the hell would Augustus go to XM's extraction site?" Gates asked.

"I have no idea," replied Milken. "Killing the extraction team serves him no good. If it is retribution he wants, they have no value towards that end."

"Unless…" responded Gates.

"Unless what?" asked Milken.

"Those XM boys are known to no one, but are tightly weaved into the fabric of our business. Augustus might be trying to use their connections to his advantage."

"And do what, Gates?" Milken queried, somewhat confused.

"Work his way through the XM chain of command, to back door his way to us." Gates replied.

Milken chewed his inner lip, considered what Gates just offered, and said, "That is way off the mark. He knows our identities, and where we are located. There is no logical reason for him to try getting at us through XM. Besides, as it relates to XM, he would only get so far. They have no reason to expose or otherwise reveal themselves to him. Frenchy was a foot soldier for them. I don't think that even he knew their chain of command."

"So, what do you propose?" asked Gates.

"I think you should call our friends in Belize, as well as E.S.C. HQ. Give them a heads up. My theory is that Augustus has snapped. An emotional breakdown of sorts. He is going to randomly kill anyone he suspects to be a participant in this entire operation. Gates, I believe wholeheartedly that this is Augustus' chosen method of suicide. He has to know that he cannot accomplish a thing going this route."

"That is pretty sad, Virg," replied Gates.

"Yeah, it is just terrible. Anyway, let me know what they say."

Milken ended the call and returned the satellite phone to the pilot. He then sat back, closed his eyes and placed his head on the padded headrest. Milken took this moment to clear his mind, whilst the whining sound of the chopper's engine and blades echoed as it sailed through the storm-filled evening sky.

⌘⌘⌘

TWO

NEBRASKA
DECEMBER 2010

The locomotive reduced its speed. It initially appeared to Augustus that the conductor did so to navigate a sharp curve. However, upon resuming a straight-line path, the train continued to slow down.

Augustus tapped his watch once to illuminate it.

"We are at least thirty minutes from Omaha," he muttered, having previously calculated how long the trip would take.

The illumination from his watch dimmed, returning the train car to total blackness.

A glow emanated from his right trouser pocket. Augustus reached in and retrieved the only item in there. It contained the device he took from the XM operative he recently killed in Des Moines, Iowa.

Augustus quickly inspected the apparatus, to determine if a communication was about to commence.

Nothing.

The device showed no further signs of activity. Without hesitation, he tossed it behind some wood planks next to him.

"They are coming," he said, sensing that the momentary glow he witnessed represented the activation of a tracking mechanism.

Augustus moved rapidly about the compartment, deciding how to best greet his boarding party.

"They will come in shooting," he said. "We are out in the middle of nowhere, and away from witnesses."

Augustus tapped his watch again, and pointed the brightness it emitted upward. He saw a sliver of space where he could hide. He then scurried up the train car's wall, utilizing its protruding ridges to propel himself. Just as he settled into his ambush position, he heard a distinct, metallic sound.

"Gas," said Augustus, recognizing the characteristically sharp chink of someone opening gas canisters.

෴෴෴

Someone forcefully opened the train car door from the outside. Simultaneously, several clankety-clank sounds reverberated throughout the compartment, as canisters of noxious gas tumbled within it.

Despite stormy weather, the night's full moon introduced clarity into the now exposed compartment. However, it was short-lived.

A thick, white phosphor quickly occupied every crevice of the compartment, just as four mercenaries, armed with submachine guns and donning gas masks, swiftly boarded.

One of the men looked at something in his hand. He then pointed to where Augustus tossed the device just moments before.

In response, the mercenaries rapidly shot their weapons several times in that direction.

The man who pointed to that spot was the group's leader. He raised his hand, and the shooting stopped.

The thick cloud of gas did not dissipate, nor would it for several more minutes.

The leader inched forward into the compartment, to confirm their kill. He got as far as he could go. He did not see a body. Hurriedly, he pressed a button on the gadget he held. The device he sought illuminated behind some wood planks.

Alarmed, the leader quickly retreated to alert his team.

෴෴෴

White, dense smoke condensed on the leader's goggles, obstructing his vision as he walked through the train car. He came to the end of the abyss, by the train door's opening, and saw a figure.

He wiped his goggles while saying, "The target is not with the device. We must search the rest of the compartment for him."

"There is no need to do that," replied the figure in front of him. "I am right here."

The lead mercenary uncharacteristically froze from astonishment, just steps from Augustus, who spoke while holding a long knife. A large amount of blood dripped from it onto the floor.

What shocked the lead mercenary even more was that Augustus was not wearing a gas mask.

After years of ingesting recombinant DNA drugs, administered to him by NICO so that he could complete missions in highly toxic environments, Augustus was impervious to most chemical warfare agents.

Augustus wiped the blood from the knife onto his right pant leg. He then pointed it at the lead mercenary, saying, "I have something you want, and vice versa. Your men are all dead. How do you wish to proceed?"

The leader responded by raising his weapon.

Augustus, holding the knife in his right hand, addressed this threat by quickly drawing his pistol with his left, shooting once.

The bullet tore into the lead mercenary's dominant shoulder, causing him to drop his weapon.

Augustus continued his assault by shooting the man once in each kneecap.

The lead mercenary plummeted to the compartment floor, letting out a shrill scream.

Augustus closed the distance between them in a flash. As he did, he retrieved the jackpot lottery ticket from his shirt pocket. He held it out, saying, "I believe this is what you are looking for."

He then stabbed the lead mercenary once in the right thigh, just for good measure. Augustus needed answers, and time was not on his side.

The man answered affirmatively by gesturing with a rushed nod, as he continued to shriek in pain.

The question is, thought Augustus, looking at the man, *did you know in advance that I was here, or did you intend on killing the original courier? If that is the case, you have no clue as to my identity.*

అ అ అ

Augustus leaned forward and slowly wiped both sides of the once again blood-soaked blade across the man's forehead. He then whispered, "I want to give you the dignity of being killed with a clean knife."

The antic had the desired effect on the man. It instituted an uncontrollable primal fear within him.

The mercenary's voice was raspy, the result of decades of smoking non-filtered cigarettes, as well as from the sudden development of blood in his throat. "E...S...C...is on their way here now."

The man looked at the device he previously held, now on the floor next to him.

Augustus picked it up, and said, "This is what you used to find me, correct?"

The man tried to say yes, but coughed up blood instead.

"Will they use this to extract you as well?"

"Yes, yes," gurgled the lead mercenary, moaning.

Augustus eyed the man and studied his wardrobe. *This man is a professional.* He then looked at the would-be assassin in his eyes. *He is intelligent, too, and probably lives by a code of conduct.*

Augustus backed away slightly and said, "You will die here. You know this, correct?"

The man nodded in the affirmative while looking at Augustus straight in his eyes.

"Are you a man of honor, or are you a mere soldier of fortune?" Augustus queried, half-knowing the answer.

"HONOR!" the man shouted, spitting blood in every direction with the utterance.

"Then one question will decide whether you die with honor or with disgrace," Augustus said coldly before asking, "Who am I?"

Confused, the man slowly replied, "The courier seeking E.S.C. extraction."

A smile emanated across Augustus' face, as he briefly looked away, reflecting on the man's answer. *They do not know I am here.* He then scrutinized the suffering lead mercenary. *He did not come here to kill ME. My anger and retribution do not apply to this man.*

Augustus shuffled closer to the man and said, "If you are a man of faith, and want to say a prayer, the time is now."

"I already have."

Without hesitation, Augustus placed his handgun to the man's forehead, and pulled the trigger.

The lead mercenary's body slumped peacefully onto its final resting place.

Augustus placed the device in his pocket. He then jumped from the train car into the vast, cold Nebraska badlands beyond.

⌘⌘⌘

THREE

A stealthy, black chopper zoomed through severe storm clouds, high in the Nebraska sky. Forty-five minutes had elapsed since the pilot departed his base, located deep in the Black Hills of South Dakota. Powerful gusts of wind created an unsettling level of turbulence upon the aircraft, periodically setting off warning sounds. The pilot checked the control panel's dials to determine structural and system stability.

"Mother of God," exclaimed the pilot. "I'm the one who is going to need an emergency extraction with this weather."

The chopper's communication system crackled, followed by a female voice. "Black Cat September, this is Pine Watch. What is your status, over?"

"Pine Watch, this is Black Cat September. Status is green, and so am I. This storm is shaking me around like a maraca!" He looked at the dashboard screen. "It says here that I am fifteen-minutes from the signal, over."

"That is a copy, Black Cat September. Please provide an update upon recovery. Pine Watch, out."

"10-4," replied the pilot. He then settled in for the remaining portion of his supersonic flight.

❧❧❧

"**D**o you understand what you are saying to me?" Gates shouted to the emergency services dispatch officer.

"Sir," the dispatch officer offered in response, "if you would, please, try to understand."

"I understand full well. Don't you dare patronize me," snapped Gates, "YOU are the one who is having a problem with comprehension. Your pilot is heading straight into an ambush. The courier you intend on extracting is dead, and the man who murdered him is waiting for you assholes to pick him up!"

The dispatch officer understood Gates' concerns. However, he was privy to information unavailable to Gates. Namely, that the pilot was extracting a team sent to kill the courier. Consequently, the dispatch officer felt confident that the team would effectively neutralize whoever stood in place of the original courier. Unfortunately, these were facts he could not share with Gates. Instead, he had to purport an inability to communicate with the pilot, due to mandatory protocols governing these extractions.

"Young man," offered Gates, "mandates are not absolute. There are times that require you to operate outside the lines to save your ass. This is one of those times. There is a zip in the wire, and you had better do all you can to contain it, or you will have hell to pay. I can promise you that."

"I'm sorry, sir. I cannot do anything more. I can assure you we have protocols in place to address the threats you speak of."

"You are going to need more than a goddamned protocol in order to deal with what is headed your way," replied Gates, ending the conversation.

అఎఎఎ

Augustus wandered aimlessly across the frost-covered field, just beyond the locomotive. He did not know where the E.S.C. extraction would take place.

Maybe I acted hastily in killing the man before asking him for the extraction point, he thought, scanning the intense darkness around him.

"I hope they actually use this thing to find me," he grumbled, looking at the contraption he took from the mercenary.

He continued trekking at a slow and steady pace, giving thought to what he was trying to accomplish.

"Retribution," he muttered. He then reflected on the events that led him to this dark, cold, and maddening place.

NICO, Milken, and the rest of those bastards...I can easily find all of them. I know them, and I know their faces. They will not escape my wrath. However, XM is a different story altogether.

Augustus stopped, and looked skyward. He thought he heard something. He remained motionless with eager anticipation, but nothing happened. He resumed his stride and continued with his thoughts.

XM is a phantom. Even when I was an active operative, I only heard of their existence, but never met anyone within their ranks, not that I was aware of anyway. How does one hunt phantoms?

Augustus paused and pursed his lips, while touching the jackpot lottery ticket in his trousers.

"You don't. Instead, you manipulate the phantoms to make them emerge from their realm to hunt you."

A swoosh sound, followed by a rapid shift in temperature, caught his attention.

"Something has just disturbed the immediate airspace around me," he said. "The extraction is here."

Augustus stopped walking, kept his eyes skyward and cautiously crouched as low as he could go.

ॐॐॐ

A deep and loud sequence of beeping filled the chopper's cabin. The source of the noise was a button labelled, CONFIRM.

The pilot pressed the button once. It turned green, and the beeping stopped.

"Okay, let's get you guys loaded up so we can boogie on out of here," mused the pilot. His orders were simple and clear. Extract a team of four and hustle them to the Canadian border, where an Airbus awaited the mercenaries.

The pilot lowered the craft, and gently touched it down. Upon landing, its side door slid open, revealing a dark interior. The pilot then signaled an 'all clear' to what he believed was an awaiting team. He did so by flicking on the interior lights twice, in rapid succession.

ॐॐॐ

Although he could barely see it, Augustus knew an aircraft was landing. The near silence of the aircraft, and its low visibility, impressed Augustus. He contemplated the best method to proceed, and wondered about the number of personnel on board. Suddenly, the aircraft's interior lights lit up, twice. This startled Augustus, but provided him with the answers he sought.

"The passenger compartment is empty," he said. "It will only be me and maybe a pilot or two." Augustus stood up and made a beeline dash to the mysterious aircraft.

The pilot flinched slightly upon Augustus' headfirst dive into the chopper. "Woah now, ease up," he said, "you are gonna wreck yourself crashing into stuff like that."

Augustus scanned the compartment and asked, "No co-pilot?"

"Negative. It is just me." The pilot then glanced outside, through the open door. "Are the other three coming today or are they having a grand ole' time out there?"

"They are not coming," said Augustus, "they are all dead. It is just me. We must leave quickly."

"Holy buckets!" cried the pilot, "what the hell did you boys get into? No need to tell me, we are up and away."

The helicopter rose quickly and sped northward.

The pilot activated the communications system and reported his status. "Pine Watch, this is Black Cat September, do you copy?"

Augustus listened to the exchange intently for any indication of danger.

"Black Cat September, this is Pine Watch. We do copy, over."

"Pine Watch, extraction is complete, minus three personnel killed in action. We are on course to the Canuck drop point, over."

"Black Cat September, please confirm your report on KIAs, over."

"Roger, Pine Watch. Extraction consisted of one team member. He reports that the other three died in the operation, over."

There was a slight pause. "Roger, Black Cat September. Continue to the drop point. Have the team member confirm possession of the item with the client, over."

"10-4 Pine Watch. Black Cat September, out."

The pilot reached to the far right of the control panel and detached a gadget from it.

Augustus eyed his every move with great suspicion.

The pilot dismissively handed the apparatus over his shoulder to Augustus. "Here, you know what to do with this. They need confirmation that you have what you came here for."

"Do you know what I came here for?" Augustus asked, gauging the pilot's level of operational intelligence.

"I am on a need-to-know basis, and don't need to know a damn thing. Moreover, I don't want to know, so don't tell me."

The pilot was emphatic in his response. Augustus was convinced he had no role here other than to fly.

"Very well," said Augustus, "silence between us it shall be." He then feigned competence in operating the gadget the pilot just handed to him and thought, *What the fuck do I do now?*

⌘⌘⌘

FOUR

C. Virgil Milken ordinarily handled himself professionally, in accordance with his role as Director of NICO. There were instances, however, where his penchant for analytical reasoning went out the window, replaced by pure rage.

Milken currently found himself embroiled in such an occurrence.

"What in God's name, Gates, does E.S.C. think they are up against?" Milken shouted, responding to Gates' briefing on his conversation with the dispatch officer.

"I thought the same thing, Virg," replied Gates. "It seems to me like they are being rather cavalier about whole thing."

"E.S.C. has protocols in place to handle these situations? Is that what they said to you, Gates?"

"That is affirmative, Virg. They did not seem concerned at all."

"What about XM?" Milken asked. "What was their response?"

"None," answered Gates. "I could not get through to them."

"I will get to the bottom of this nonsense with XM in due time. But for right now, I am not buying the answer E.S.C. gave you," said Milken. "E.S.C. does not handle these types of emergencies. They may have a security team or two, but that is about it. We have already witnessed Augustus decimate our highly specialized assets. Those soy boys at E.S.C. will pose no challenge to whatever plan Augustus has up his sleeve."

"I agree, Virg. What do you suggest we do next?"

Milken instructed Gates to hold on while he spoke with his pilot.

Gates acquiesced.

"Pilot," said Milken, "how long before we arrive at our destination?"

"Two hours and twenty-four minutes, sir."

"Where are we right now?" Milken asked.

"We are just south of the Iowa border, sir, in Missouri."

Milken thought for a moment, and said, "Pilot, I need you to put me down in Lee's Summit, Missouri. The Grotto…if you know where that is located."

The pilot began to retort. "Sir, I have orders to…"

The sound of Milken chambering a round into his 9mm handgun startled the pilot. His reaction caused the helicopter to swerve slightly.

Milken did not say a word.

The pilot broke the uneasy silence, and said, "The Grotto, aye, sir, Lee's Summit, Missouri. ETA is thirty-two minutes."

"Speed it up," ordered Milken. "We don't have time for a fucking joy ride."

He then returned to his phone call with Gates.

"That sounded rather intense," said Gates.

"These pathetic E.S.C. pilots," replied Milken, agitated. "They are nothing but a bunch of prima donnas. That is my point though, Gates. E.S.C. does not have the backbone necessary to deal with a threat like Peña. Something else is going on, and I intend on finding out what that is."

Milken instructed Gates to have NICO security units meet him at The Grotto, and ended the call.

"When we get there," Milken growled at the pilot, "take off and go back to your hiding place. I won't need your sorry ass anymore."

The pilot did not respond, nor did he utter a sound throughout the remaining minutes of their flight.

෧෧෧

The Midwestern State of Missouri dubbed the "cave state," is home to over 4,500 known wild, natural caves. It has more caverns than any other state in America.

In addition to these wonders of nature, Missouri houses several vast networks of industrial, manmade caves under various cities and towns.

The city of Lee's Summit is home to one of these massive complexes.

Nestled deep within the labyrinth of carved out limestone snaking underneath Lee's Summit, exists an 82,000 square foot facility known affectionately in the clandestine community as The Grotto.

Known to the public as the Federal Records Center, it boasts as being the first underground National Archives installation.

Far from being a records center, The Grotto serves as the nation's primary weapon in the war on terror. The sprawling complex is abuzz twenty-four hours a day, as supercomputers operated by robotic soldiers compartmentalize terabytes of cell phone, internet and other private communications data utilizing methods not sanctioned under U.S. law.

Although NICO had no official role with operations at The Grotto, the nature of their missions meshed perfectly with this installation's framework. Consequently, NICO enjoyed unfettered access to this futuristic colony of robotic legionnaires, and relied on their support often.

ॐॐॐ

Per Milken's instructions, the helicopter arrived alongside a quarry, just beyond the cave's entrance. A yawning, black-mouthed limestone mine greeted them as they touched down.

Milken exited the aircraft, turned to the pilot and said, "Adios," while gesturing a mock salute.

The chopper took off.

Milken looked at his watch. He knew it would be several minutes before NICO assets arrived from deep within the cave. He decided to call Gates.

"I need you to get everyone on an encrypted conference call, ASAP. Time is of the essence. I don't give a shit where they are physically located. They can be at a circus, tossing midgets for all I care, but they had better get their asses on the line. Do I make myself clear, Gates?"

"As clear as mud, Virg." Gates chuckled, as he ended the call to make the necessary arrangements.

ॐॐॐ

Milken heard a rumbling sound from his rear. He turned and saw three desert camouflaged vehicles approaching. He walked to the lead vehicle and went to the passenger side to address the occupants.

The driver jokingly said, "You need a ride, soldier?"

"You're damn right I do," replied Milken. "I need to patch into a scrambled communication. Does this hunk of crap have the proper equipment?"

"Hell," replied the old, sinewy driver, who served with Milken in Vietnam. "This here vehicle is like Puff the Magic Dragon on steroids, sir. She has all you need, and will keep your ass alive."

Milken smiled at the driver's reference to Puff the Magic Dragon. It represented the nickname that troops during the Vietnam War gave to the Douglas AC-47 Spooky; a close air support gunship that orbited pinned down soldiers for hours, providing suppression fire as well as dropping flares to illuminate the battlefield. This enabled U.S. forces to have a fighting chance at surviving relentless onslaughts on their positions by an oftentimes unseen enemy.

Milken entered the vehicle, and went to its rear. He sat at a small console and put on a large, black helmet. He then punched an alphanumeric code into the panel before him, and waited.

A computerized voice sounded, "Name, please."

"Zulu," replied Milken.

The communication helmet he wore allowed him to talk freely, without any concern of compromise. It represented a sphere of silence. Although he spoke at full volume inside the helmet, his voice was inaudible to the outside world.

The computerized voice replied, stating, "Ocular scan in five...four...three...two...one..."

At the end of the countdown, a device lowered and stopped in front of Milken's eyes. A bright flash almost blinded Milken as it verified his identity.

"Zulu authenticated," said the computerized voice. "Please proceed."

Milken knew he had some time before everyone was able to get on the line. The inner portion of the helmet lens also served as a computer screen, with secure online access via voice commands.

Milken was curious. He wanted a visual of what he was potentially dealing with, so he issued a voice command for a map of Omaha, Nebraska.

The geographical request quickly appeared on the helmet screen. He pondered the city's coordinates for a moment, and thought, *Canada, those assholes were going to extract Frenchy and take him to Canada. They were going to get him out of the U.S. first, then return him to Belize. Those poor bastards. It is not Frenchy they are getting.*

An idea crept into Milken's head. He then issued a voice command to have a coded message sent to XM seeking a status update.

He wondered how long it would take for a reply.

It did not take long for them to respond.

"MISSION ABORTED. ASSET HAS RETURNED TO BELIZE. PAYMENTS ALREADY MADE TO OUR ACCOUNT SHALL BE CREDITED TO FUTURE OPERATIONS…END MESSAGE."

"Those stinking, lying, rat bastards," shouted Milken, ripping off the helmet. "Their asset returned to Belize, and nothing about an E.S.C. extraction? What is it that they are trying to hide?"

Milken put the helmet back on, and called Gates.

"Hold off on the conference call, Gates. I am ending this right now. The gloves are coming off for good. The nerve of those pricks is astounding. They not only avoid their commitment to us, but then they lie to us about it!"

"Did you confront them with their lie, and inform them about Augustus being on that chopper, instead of their asset?" Gates asked.

"No. They can go to Hell," replied Milken.

"But XM still believes that their asset is alive in the United States, in need of an extraction. What are you going to do?" Gates asked, sounding a bit concerned.

"I am going to place XM in check," he replied. "Not only am I going to accomplish the mission of killing Augustus, but I will also ensure that XM believes I sacked their asset, as payback for them lying to us. We will regain the respect we deserve from them."

ॐ ॐ ॐ

Frank Newberry was the Director for Internal Matters at the National Security Agency. His position was largely unknown to those outside the beltway. Nevertheless, his power to conduct operations within the United States was without limit, and beyond reproach.

It was 3:30am in Washington, DC. However, Director Newberry was not at home at this late hour. Instead, he was in his oversized, antique-laden office, finishing a romp with one of his regular escorts on his expensive, yet comfortable, leather couch.

"Questo è per te, mia cara," he said to the woman in perfect Italian, stating that he had something for her. He then handed her an envelope full of one hundred dollar bills.

The stunningly beautiful woman smiled seductively at him, slowly wiped her lips, and exited his office.

Director Newberry began to retreat into the private bath in his office when the phone rang.

"Go ahead," he said, after placing the receiver to his ear.

"It's Milken."

"What are you doing calling me at this hour?"

"Well, for starters, I'm not doing anything near as fun as you," joked Milken.

Newberry looked around his office, expecting to find a camera pointed directly at him.

"Don't bother. There are no cameras in your office. You are just very predictable." Milken chuckled softly as he spoke.

"Are you calling to bust my balls, or do you have a meaningful reason for dialing me up?"

"I...well, actually, WE have a very serious problem on our hands that requires immediate attention, and I mean pronto." Milken replied.

"I'm sorry," retorted Newberry. "I fail to see how a NICO problem becomes mine. We are organized separately for a reason, or did you forget?"

"Look asshole," shouted Milken. "One of our most potent assets ever has gone off the reservation. He is armed with names, times and places, and is prepared to reveal it all to whoever will listen to him. This is larger than NICO. In fact, it is even larger than the NSA. This individual has the potential to singlehandedly rewrite history, while turning our allies against us in a flash."

"Well, if this is such a big deal, Milken, then why haven't we had some indication of it within the public sphere? I mean, even the most secretive of missions have some sort of disinformation in the media, to explain away certain suspicious events."

"There has been," replied Milken. "I take it you haven't caught the news reports out of Iowa?"

Newberry laughed loudly. "What, the winning lottery ticket? Is that the big buzz on all of this?"

"Did you just say a winning lottery ticket? Jesus, what is wrong with you? Did that prostitute screw away what was left of your brains?" Milken snorted. "No, the carjacking attempt; bombs going off; a political appointee targeted and missing. If you would just spend less time with…oh my God. Lottery, really?"

"Alright, alright," said Newberry. "I might have heard something about that too. So, are you saying that those events are directly connected to your issue?"

Milken confirmed, and described his plan of action in detail.

Newberry raised his eyebrows high, reflecting his astonishment at Milken's bold proposal.

"I don't see how we can…" Newberry started to say, but Milken interrupted.

"Make it happen, Director Newberry, or we are all doomed."

⌘⌘⌘

FIVE

Augustus examined the gadget that the pilot handed him. He expected there to be a button, or some other type of mechanism for him to engage to communicate.

What will I say? Will they recognize my voice as not belonging to one of their men? Augustus pondered.

The device came to life on its own, and its thin screen began populating with words.

Out of curiosity, Augustus touched the screen. Instantly, the gadget's exterior expanded sideways, revealing a full, smartphone-like keyboard.

Fantastic, thought Augustus. *I do not need to speak.*

The words along the screen were simple, and formulated a straightforward question. "Do you have the item?"

"Yes," typed Augustus. He observed that there existed zero room for error in the architecture of this device.

The gizmo had no 'send' feature, and no method to correct an entry. It went live into the feed the moment he typed. *They are capturing my initial thoughts, with no opportunity for editing my response. I have no doubt they are also timing how long I take to reply.*

"Good," was the response on the gadget. Followed by, "Please identify the item."

Augustus typed without hesitation. "A lottery ticket, named Hot Ticket, from the state of Iowa."

"Did you verify its status?"

"Negative," replied Augustus. "The situation which led to multiple KIA's prevented such vetting."

"Please provide the numbers from the ticket, as well as the drawing date."

Augustus complied. He typed all six numbers from the ticket and furnished the drawing date associated with it.

Thirty seconds elapsed. It felt like an eternity to Augustus. The crawler then read, "Verification complete. Proceed to the secondary drop-zone. You are to inform the pilot of the updated coordinates. Our next communication will be upon your arrival at that location."

The device then lost all signs of activity.

Augustus pondered his next move, as he peered out the chopper's window. *Secondary drop zone? I have no idea where that could be. I have gone as far as I can on this route. They will learn my identity due to my inability to inform the pilot of the new coordinates. It is time for me to pursue those XM bastards in other ways.*

ॐॐॐ

Newberry returned the phone to its base after ending his conversation with Milken. He felt perturbed, if not downright distraught, with what he just learned.

Although clothed with incredible powers to conduct operations he deemed necessary to preserve the country's national security, he occasionally obtained advice and guidance from other administrators, such as Milken.

He felt extremely uneasy about this mission. However, he had no reason to suspect Milken's intentions…a man whom he held in the highest regard.

Newberry ran his long, manicured fingers through his thick, curly hair, and stormed off to the bathroom to take a shower.

"First things first," he said aloud as he stomped across the office floor. "I need to clean that whore off me so that I can think clearly."

ॐॐॐ

United States Air Force Lieutenant Colonel Ben "Taco" Virgin sat down in his office to eat. On his plate were leftovers from his favorite Mexican fast-food restaurant. He was about to chow it down when his office door opened.

"Sir," said a young aviator, currently off rotation from his primary duty as a drone sensor operator. "A package has just arrived for you by courier."

"Who in their right mind delivers a package at this hour?" demanded Virgin. "Do you know who it is from?"

"The courier is with NSA, sir."

Virgin stood up, and motioned with his hands for the young man to show the courier in.

He complied and returned just moments later.

"We will take it from here," said Virgin to the sensor operator, who promptly left the office, and shut the door.

"The agency has an urgent request, requiring immediate action," said the tall, muscular NSA agent.

"What's in the package?" Virgin asked, glancing at a box the agent held in his hands.

"The only method you will use to communicate with us." He placed the box on Virgin's desk, and said - "I'd open it right now if I were you. Time is ticking."

Virgin frowned slightly, and stepped to the box. He opened it and saw what looked like a motorcycle helmet. He looked at the agent and said, "Really?"

The agent did not respond. Instead, he looked straight into Virgin's eyes with a deadpan expression.

Virgin reached into the box and retrieved the contraption. He held it out in front of him with both hands. He inspected it and said, "Well, shit, I guess I'll just put this bad boy on."

Upon placing it over his head, the inside of the device lit up, and a screen appeared before his eyes.

"Can you see me?" Director Newberry asked.

"Uh, yeah, crystal clear," replied Virgin, somewhat confused. He had met Newberry several times at various closed-door congressional briefings.

"Good," said Newberry. "I can see you too. Now, let us get down to business." Newberry pointed to a large digital clock behind him that was counting backwards. "Do you see that clock?"

"I do," replied Virgin.

"That clock represents the amount of time you have to perform your duty. If you fail, you will die. I am sorry for being so blunt about it but, as you can see, you really do not have much time."

Virgin felt an extreme chill overcome him. He did not know what to say, or how to react.

"Okay, now that I have your undivided attention, I will provide you with your mission. There is a chopper headed, we presume, to the Canadian border, via the Dakotas. You must destroy it before it reaches its destination."

"I am not authorized to fly armed drones over U.S. soil. You know that!" Virgin shouted.

Newberry looked over his shoulder, towards the clock, and looked back at Virgin, without saying a word.

Virgin pleaded, "That clock says fifty-five minutes. How can I - ?"

Newberry interrupted him. "You have drones stationed at Offutt Air Force Base in Bellevue, Nebraska, correct? They can intercept within minutes. Do it."

"I can lose my command if I do this," protested Virgin.

"Perhaps," replied Newberry. "But, you will lose your life if you do not." He then said, "The chopper's exact location will be provided to you once you get your drone airborne."

ॐॐॐ

Lieutenant Colonel Virgin ripped the helmet off his head and stared at the NSA agent with a horrified look.

The agent did not flinch.

Virgin suddenly sensed that if he did not jump into action at this very moment, this man would tear him into pieces. Virgin did not hesitate and bolted out his office with the helmet device.

"Come with me," Virgin ordered the young sensor operator. "You are back on rotation and supporting my flight mission."

The young man was about to say something, but Virgin did not let him.

"Don't you open your goddamned mouth, you hear me? We are code red, and are going weapons hot."

The sensor operator's eyes grew wide, and slowly turned to the large, intimidating NSA agent.

"Don't look at him. Hey, hey, look at me! Don't you even think about looking at him again, you got that? Now, let's go. Flight Raptor Six is away from all flight teams currently on duty.

We should be in and out of there in under thirty minutes. Move it!"

The two men double-timed their pace to the drone command area known as Flight Raptor Six.

By contrast, the NSA agent walked coolly, as he followed them across the base.

In the United States Air Force, the drone pilot corps consists of two groups: pilots and sensor operators. The drones, typically referred to as Remotely Piloted Aircraft or RPA, are operated from various locations around the globe, in what are known as RPA workstations. Flight Raptor Six was located on an air base that housed several of these workstations.

As the drone pilot, Virgin was to fly the aircraft, while the sensor operator controlled numerous cameras.

Upon entering Flight Raptor Six, Virgin flicked on the necessary dials to bring the workstation to life. After determining that everything was operational, Virgin settled into the pilot seat, alongside his visibly nervous sensor operator.

The two men looked briefly into each other's eyes, then turned to look straight ahead.

In front of them were multiple computer screens of various sizes. For drone crews, multitasking was the norm. Customarily, they would communicate with other crews operating within their theatre of combat via text messages, but not today. On this mission, they would be the only crew operating an armed RPA over U.S. soil.

The NSA agent arrived at the workstation several minutes after Virgin and his sensor operator. He waited for the crew to settle in. He then approached Virgin.

"Here are your coordinates, sir."

Virgin took the thick piece of paper from him, and read the details. He briefly glanced up at the agent, then shifted his focus to the sensor operator.

"Here, read this once and memorize it." Virgin ordered.

"Copy that, sir," the sensor operator replied.

"Are we good, gentlemen?" asked the agent.

"As good as we will ever be," replied Virgin.

The sensor operator mouthed an affirmation to the agent while simultaneously, and cautiously, nodding his head.

"Good," said the agent. "Then get your bird aloft, and on task."

The drone crew reacted swiftly to the agent's directive. Within moments, they put the heavily armed Nebraska based RPA into the air, and on the hunt.

のののの

Augustus contemplated his options, to include forcing the pilot to land and, if necessary, killing him. He did not know the coordinates for a secondary landing zone. His identity was at serious risk of exposure.

"Pilot," shouted Augustus, intending on ordering him to land the chopper.

However, just as the pilot began to respond, a deafening beep emitted from the aircraft's speakers.

Simultaneously, the XM gadget that Augustus held buzzed in rapid succession.

Augustus prepared for the worst.

Due to the noise, the pilot had to shout into his communication radio. "Come again, Pine Watch. I did not copy that message, over."

"Black Cat September be advised that a major storm surge will prevent you from pushing to the intended drop zone. You will need to rally instead at one, five, two, Lima in fifteen mikes, over."

Augustus listened to this exchange as he read the XM message coming through on his device. "The plan for secondary drop zone is aborted. You will experience treacherous weather ahead. Rendezvous at E.S.C. drop point with locally embedded assets."

"Copy that, Pine Watch," continued the pilot. "I am re-coordinating our flight path to one, five, two, Lima. This is Black Cat September, out."

Locally embedded assets? Augustus thought. *What in the hell does that mean? Does that mean sleeper XM operators? Does that mean someone from NICO will greet me? Will Milken be there?*

These and many other thoughts rushed through Augustus' head. The possibilities of whom he would be meeting were endless.

Maybe there really is no storm surge, and this is just a ploy to ambush me. I must act at once.

"Pilot," shouted Augustus, waving the XM device in the air as he spoke. "You will be putting us down in just under fifteen minutes, correct?"

"That is affirmative, sir."

"Outstanding. I have orders for you to put me down five minutes before your scheduled touchdown. I will hump the rest of the way in."

The pilot turned towards Augustus and gave him an inquisitive look.

"Sorry, but this is what my people need to happen," said Augustus. "Pine Watch has not been notified, for security purposes. Consequently, you will not be able to verify this directive with them. I am sure you can understand."

The pilot shrugged, turned away from Augustus and said, "That's fine with me. I am not the one trying to get the heck out of Dodge. I will locate a clearing about five minutes from the drop zone, and put you down. I will also wait five minutes after that point to inform my command that you needed out sooner. You know, to give you a head start."

The pilot smiled, like a kid who just said something clever. He then resumed his concentration on flying.

Something about the pilot's smile reminded Augustus of his son. He longed to see Nathaniel again, to hold him, smell him, and kiss his soft skin.

Augustus shook his head slightly. He could not let the sorrow and the pain distract him. He was about to converge upon a potentially lethal moment, and needed to be as sharp as ever.

৯৯৯

The weather deteriorated greatly, causing enormous stress upon the aircraft. The interior of the chopper echoed with the sounds of hard-working engines, and rotor blades. It became so loud that Augustus, and the pilot, could no longer hear each other speak.

The pilot reached above his head for some controls. Simultaneously, he looked at Augustus and motioned for him to put on the headset hanging next to him.

Augustus complied and the pilot began to speak.

"This storm is a killer," said the pilot, shaking his head while laughing. "I'm coming up on your exit in about another three minutes. Get your shit together for a quick withdrawal. It probably would be wise if Pine Watch did not notice that I stopped. So, as I figure it, you will need to drop and roll from about eight feet. Are you okay with that?"

"I'm pretty sure that I can handle it," replied Augustus.

The pilot acknowledged, "Roger, I'm dropping in now. Be ready to move."

Moments later, the pilot nodded and gave Augustus the thumbs up, while saying, "Okay, time for you to get out."

Augustus placed his hand on the pilot's shoulder and said, "Thank you. This is a great favor. I will never forget." He then removed the headset, slid open the chopper's door, and jumped out.

After dropping approximately eight feet to the ground, Augustus landed and rolled effortlessly into a kneeling position. He remained motionless, to gather his bearings. Something caught his attention. It was a sound, a very troubling sound.

The storm's gusts howled into his ears. In addition to the winds, Augustus could hear the thumping of helicopter blades, as the aircraft regained its altitude. However, these sounds were not what caught his attention. What did catch his attention was a steady, fizzing sound.

It grew louder by the nanosecond.

The sound morphed into a fizzing crackle, as it got closer.

Augustus looked skyward, towards the rising helicopter. His heart stopped when he saw what approached it.

From the rear of the helicopter advanced two cylindrical shaped, phosphorous-like tubes of smoke. They each contained a bright flame within them.

"Oh, no," said a stunned Augustus, recognizing the formations as belonging to missiles.

The helicopter stood no chance of survival. The two plumes of smoke closed in on it, like a pair of great white sharks going in for the kill of an unsuspecting prey.

Upon impact, the chopper appeared to stop moving. Its interior lit up, followed by an intense orange and reddish glow.

Augustus reached towards the chopper, as if he could somehow save the pilot and the aircraft from what was to come.

"NO!" he screamed.

The power of the storm's winds paled in comparison to the eruption of the blast that followed. Instantly, the helicopter disappeared into a hellacious fireball.

Augustus witnessed the destruction through his outstretched hands.

Although dangerously close to the exploding chopper, he did not dive for cover. Instead, Augustus looked straight at this fireball of destruction and shrieked a painful cry at the top of his lungs.

He then fell forward, and remained on his hands and knees, as the chopper plummeted onto the frozen prairie below.

࿅࿅࿅

"Target destroyed," said the sensor operator.

Lieutenant Colonel Virgin did not reply. Instead, he stared blankly at the screen in front of him, observing the destructive blast.

"Sir?" pressed the sensor operator, seeking some form of response.

"Copy that," Virgin finally said. "I'm bringing her home."

The drone crew returned the RPA to its Nebraska airbase, and shut down all the systems within Flight Raptor 6. Afterwards, the two men walked back to Virgin's office, slowly, as if in a fog.

"Sir," said the sensor operator. "Where is the NSA agent?"

Virgin glanced around. He looked at the helmeted device in his hand and said, "I don't know. In fact, I am not even certain that he was in Flight Raptor 6 for the entire mission. I guess I wasn't really paying attention to him."

Upon returning to Virgin's office, the sensor operator said, "I am going to grab something to eat, if that is okay with you, sir?"

"Absolutely," replied Virgin. "You've earned a good meal. Here." Virgin reached into his pocket, pulled out his wallet and retrieved a $20 bill. "Get something on me."

The sensor operator smiled and took the bill without protest. He then thanked Virgin and exited the office.

Virgin grabbed the helmeted device, and sat down at his desk. He determined it to be best if he put on the contraption to provide a status report. However, he also felt confident that the relevant stakeholders already knew the exact details of the mission's outcome.

He put the helmet on, anticipating the same blinding flash he experienced earlier.

Nothing happened.

The screen that appeared before his eyes the last time he wore it, did not manifest. Only an eerie silence occupied the interior of the helmet.

Confused, Virgin removed the helmet.

Startled, he jumped from his chair. Sitting in front of him, in a visitor chair, was the large and intimidating NSA agent.

"Man, you about scared the burritos out of me!" Virgin said, chuckling, as he placed the helmet on his desk.

The NSA agent did not respond.

Pointing to the helmet, Virgin said, "I tried reaching out to, well, you know, to report mission status...but I could not get through."

"Just give it another few minutes to get up and running. You will be able to furnish him with a full after-action report," said the NSA agent, smirking.

"Yeah, right," replied Virgin, sensing some sarcasm from the agent. He tried not to focus on the agent's menacing demeanor.

Virgin shifted his thoughts, and changed the conversation.

"I'm hungry. Would you mind if I ate something while we wait on that thing to fire up?"

"Not at all," said the agent. "Please, enjoy your meal."

Virgin's pulse began beating rapidly. He could not put a finger on it, but he felt uneasy. His nervousness caused him to become talkative, and his voice crackled as he spoke.

"Oh, man, I have some great leftovers from this Mexican joint just off base. I would share with you, but they are simply too good. Tacos, yeah, that is what I have, a bunch of tacos. Hey, did you know that my pilot call sign is Taco? Ha, yeah! The guys know that I love tacos so much, they nicknamed me after them."

Virgin retrieved his leftovers, and un-wrapped them at his desk. "You know, normally, I would take the time to warm these puppies up in a toaster oven. However, I am way too hungry to mess with that!"

He stopped talking, and consumed two tacos that he pulled from the to-go sack.

"Mmmm, mmmm. I have some rice and beans here too that are going to be fabu– ."

Virgin could not complete his statement. He felt dizzy. His office seemed to spin at top speed right before his eyes. His ears rung from deep within, and he could feel his earlobes heat to a boiling temperature. Soon after, he felt his face flush, and the sensation of his eyes swelling shut. He started to choke, and began gasping for air.

He stumbled past the NSA agent to his office door. Gasping, wheezing, and barely able to see, Virgin came to understand his fate upon opening the door.

The young sensor operator, normally stationed at the desk just outside Virgin's office, was dead. His body leaned against the wall behind him, his brains splattered across it.

Virgin could see the gun that took the sensor operator's life, laid down beside him, suggestive of a suicide.

Virgin turned around, gulping urgently for air. As he did so, the NSA agent stepped to him and forcibly put the helmet over his head.

Instantly, a flash of light from within shone bright. Virgin could hardly see anything at this point. However, he could hear Newberry speak.

"Thank you for your loyal service, Lieutenant Colonel Virgin. You are a man of great honor, and will be spoken of well."

The NSA agent ripped the helmet off Virgin's head, and watched him plummet to the floor.

Virgin wheezed, inhaled small breaths of air, and died.

Upon Virgin's demise, the NSA agent put on the helmeted device to communicate with Newberry.

"Affirmative, sir," confirmed the NSA agent, when Newberry inquired about Virgin's demise. He then acknowledged an order that Newberry gave him, and exited the office.

৵৵৵

Newberry sat back in his large, leather couch. He then leaned towards a different device on his coffee table, and spoke into it.

"It is done. Did you copy that?"

"I did," replied Milken. "That was excellent work."

Newberry slowly rose from his couch. He then turned, ever so slightly, towards his office window. Looking out at the beautiful glow of lights that illuminated the nation's Capitol, he said, "This is going to change the course of U.S. history."

"It already has," replied Milken. "It already has."

⌘⌘⌘

SIX

"He who trusts secrets to a servant makes him his master" -
John Dryden

Milken's conversation with Newberry distressed him. He knew that the actions he forced Newberry to take risked sending the country down a dangerous path.

"Failure to take these measures," reasoned Milken, "would have yielded far graver consequences. I had no choice, it had to be done."

Milken retrieved his Sat-Com 5 device from its protective pouch. He then accessed the dedicated NICO satellite, and patched a communication into XM headquarters.

ॐॐॐ

The weather in the nation of Belize was exceptionally hot for this time of year. The humidity was unforgiving. Even the occasional breeze from the Caribbean Sea did nothing to provide relief, however temporary, to the swarms of locals and tourists lining the streets. However, as brutal as this temperature was, it paled in comparison to the heat boiling over inside XM headquarters.

Steering the helm of XM's communiqué center was a man known only as Rodrigo. He stood barely five feet in height, but was more forceful than those who towered over him.

Rodrigo clutched the apparatus in his hand so tightly that his knuckles started to bleed.

Irrespective of his anger, he remained silent as he listened to Milken speak.

"So," said Milken, wrapping up the admonishment he just laid upon Rodrigo. "Let this be a lesson to you, and your godforsaken goons. Do not ever, and I mean EVER, think that you will breach your duty to me, and simply walk away. You may be doing work within our country that we need to refrain from performing ourselves, but that does not give you free reign, amigo. We will always monitor what you do and, as I have just proven, take the necessary corrective actions when shit gets out of hand."

Milken played his best poker bluff on this conversation with XM. He knew that Augustus was on the chopper he had blown out of the sky. However, XM did not. They believed XM personnel occupied it. For Milken, this was an opportunity to inflict a punishing blow upon XM for their attempted scheme.

"Now, I don't know what in God's name crawled up your ass to prompt you into thinking that this was a good idea, but it was not. It is not, and it will never be. Do I make myself clear, Belize?"

"Si," is all that Rodrigo offered in acknowledgement, and the communication ended.

ৡৡৡ

Prentiss Gates paced nervously, pondering the outcome of the mission. He practically pounced on the phone when it rang.

"It is finally over," said a tired sounding Milken. "That wily sonofabitch really did give us a run for our money, didn't he?"

"Augustus was never one to be toyed with," offered Gates. "I, for one, am shocked that it ended this swiftly."

"Yeah, well, lay off your erection for him, Gates. He is dead. It is time for us to move past this. With Augustus gone, I can now focus on cleaning up the mess he left behind in Iowa. Newberry has an agent heading there now to take care of his sidekick, Chad Molander. That little prick cheated death once, due to Augustus' antics...but not now."

"What about afterwards?" Gates queried.

"What do you mean, afterwards? After Deputy Director Molander is dead, I am going to relax on a Greek island, away from all of this craziness."

"Hmmm...right. Well, before you go packing suntan oil for your Greek excursion, you might want to think of wrapping up the other loose ends," said Gates.

Believing he understood Gates' reference, Milken replied - "No, Gates, I have decided to give up on the family. Augustus is gone now. Anything he might have told them is of minimal consequence at this point. We'll just let them be."

"I understand, Virg," pressed Gates. "But I was not referring to his wife and child. There is still the matter of his great friend who is guarding them. You know, the Deputy U.S. Marshal. I agree that if the wife came forward, to speak about whatever Augustus told her, that her credibility would be shaky at best. People do not trust the words of those who have been through personally traumatic experiences. The public simply views them as, you know, crazy. However, a highly decorated, former U.S. Army Delta boy turned U.S. Marshal, carries a hell of a lot of weight. Especially given the family he comes from. There are an awful lot of people who give credence to all that the Baker family claims to be true. This, Virg, is the loose end that we must fix. Without doing so, it would be as if Augustus were still alive. We would be doomed."

"Well, aren't you a gung-ho, type-A killer all of a sudden?" mocked Milken. "What in the hell has gotten into you? Has all of this action stirred up some old warhorse memories?"

"Kind of," chuckled Gates. "Plus, I must admit, I received a tip on their location just fifteen minutes ago."

"This better not be some kind of joke you are playing on me," shouted Milken.

"I have not been issued a sense of humor, that I can recall anyway," replied Gates. "So, no, I am not."

"How credible is the information?"

"It is dead on. Um, no pun intended of course," said Gates. "After that last fiasco where we lost all those XM boys, I knew that I had better activate our bird dogs within the law enforcement, and intelligence communities. Sure enough, one of our sources from within the Marshals Service reached out to me."

"What did you learn?" Milken asked hurriedly.

"The source explained to me that, within the past couple of days, a lot of activity started taking place in and around their special operations headquarters in Naco, Arizona. He became suspicious, he says, when crates of supplies arrived at one of their long-range reconnaissance hangars. The final hunch came to him when he observed unfamiliar personnel arrive. They then apparently set a staging area in a part of the compound that he does not have unfettered access to."

"So, is that it?" Milken asked, sounding somewhat disappointed.

"No, Virg, there's more. There is plenty more," replied a frustrated Gates. "The source informed me that he intended on placing a small GPS tracking device on one of those crates, so that we could learn their exact whereabouts once they departed the compound."

"That was nice of him," snorted Milken.

"Just kindhearted is all he is. However, as it turns out, with all the activity going on, and his restricted access to the staging area, he could not accomplish that for us."

"Damn, that would have been perfect," said Milken.

"I agree," replied Gates. "I do think though, Virg, that there exists another opportunity for us. Yet, it is one that has an extremely tight window for execution."

"And what is that?"

"The source tells me that the crates and the mysterious personnel have all departed. However, it appears as if a medical team is now mobilizing. Apparently, a specialized medical helicopter has recently arrived."

"I suppose it is possible that this is related to an entirely separate operation. However, the details you describe are exactly what we should expect to see as it relates to protecting, and providing medical care, to the Peña family. Gates, we need to get assets on that chopper, ASAP!" Milken shouted.

"I already took the initiative," assured Gates. "I figured that if you did not agree, you would have given me an order to abort."

"Great job, Gates! Are you outsourcing this?"

"No. We are going internal on this one. I have dispatched the Aardvarks. I am of the feeling that since we started this, then it is only appropriate we finish it too."

"I feel good about this," said Milken. "Keep me posted."

ॐॐॐ

Hector Quiñones, the source Gates spoke of, was a logistics officer within the U.S. Marshal's Service, and was charged with the duty of getting agency special operations up and running in a timely, and efficient manner. Yet, irrespective of his position, he was not privy to the events unfolding on his base, known within the U.S. Marshal's Service as Apache South.

The directive from Gates was clear. Quiñones was to get a NICO ops team, which was already in route to Apache South, aboard the medical chopper. However, this was no easy task. Quiñones would have to work smart, and fast.

"Whatever is taking place here at Apache South has got to be a Black Operations Protective Service (BOPS) mission," Quiñones said softly. "I have heard tales of how they not only provide protection from international bounty hunters and assassins, but essentially rebirth informants and their families by faking their deaths, and reintroducing them into the world with no possible connection to their previous lives. Some of the stories I have heard go well beyond that, suggesting that BOPS will assassinate anyone who might have learned of an informant's new identity. Yet, most everyone has followed up those tales by saying BOPS' existence is a myth, and is nothing more than an urban legend."

Quiñones scratched his head, pondering everything he had seen to this point. He then factored in his lack of involvement with any logistical planning, or operational details.

Finally, he assessed his instincts against NICOs "watch alert" for any sudden, unexplained activity designed to remove subjects permanently from the grid.

"This smells like the fabled BOPS to me," he muttered, thinking through his plan. "I had better watch my ass, and tread lightly."

≈≈≈

Quiñones was amazed at how quickly the NICO Aardvarks arrived at his office.

"Damn, that was quick. Send them in," he told his secretary when she called to announce their arrival.

A team of seven operatives entered his office.

Quiñones was a bit stunned at their lack of equipment. "I expected you guys to be armed to the teeth," he opined.

A female operative, named Milagros, stepped forward and replied, "We are Aardvarks, punk, and we are ready to rumble. Also, do I look like a guy?"

Sheepish, Quiñones backtracked quickly. "No, of course not, I, um, I just assumed."

Milagros interrupted his stammered response and said, "You are supposed to sneak us onto that medical helo, aren't you? How do you suppose it would look if we were packing heavy weapons, pendejo?"

"Okay," replied Quiñones. "That is fair, I suppose. I apologize. Obviously, you are not in a good mood. Let's just get to doing this."

"There is nothing about killing that makes for a good day. So, yeah, let's get this going," said a different operative.

Quiñones thought - *What did I stumble into? I was probably better off not calling in the tip. Now, I have these assholes to deal with as my reward.*

Quiñones addressed the team, "Alright, listen up. I was able to get some insight into what is going on with the medical chopper. This information was shared with me by the Chief Medical Flight Officer, who is a good friend of mine. This is what we have as our situation. There is a medical team on standby at the hangar, awaiting a final order to board. From whom, exactly, I do not know. However, what I do know is that they are non-combat oriented, i.e., doctors and nurses. There are three doctors and three nurses. There is also, of course, the pilot, who is presumably armed. There is no co-pilot on this craft. Also presumed is that the first chopper, which took off with crates of supplies, carried heavily armed BOPS personnel. Ostensibly, their mission is to secure your targets."

Quiñones further explained the role of BOPS, and the mythical nature of their existence within the Marshal's Service.

"When is that final order expected to be given?" Milagros asked.

"They are ready to go now. Luckily, the final order is contingent upon my clearing the drugs they are transporting. During my conversation with the Chief Medical Flight Officer, I reminded her that, in all her haste with putting together the medical operation, she did not log out medicines and other hazardous materials from our inventory. As any competent medical professional would, she appreciated the logistical and practical need for a chain of custody record. I assured her that the review would be quick, and efficient. When she asked me how I intended on accomplishing such a feat, I informed her that I enlisted the services of our locally stationed DEA Quality Control brethren to assist."

Quiñones exhaled in an exaggerated manner, saying, "And that would be you."

Running a hand over his chin, Quiñones said, "So, that will get you access to the crew. How you get onto that chopper is up to you."

"Sounds good to me," said Milagros. "Let's get it on then, shall we?"

࠾࠾࠾

The air hangar was approximately three hundred yards from Quiñones' office. The seven Aardvarks maintained an even pace behind Quiñones as they walked towards it. The operatives wore identical, unassuming attire that consisted of khaki slacks, black boots, and neatly tucked black polo shirts, which revealed their excellent physiques.

When they arrived, Quiñones raised his hand, signaling them to stop.

The group complied.

Quiñones approached the medical helicopter, and addressed the pilot who was leaning up against it. "Where is the Chief Medical Flight Officer?"

"I saw her heading to the hangar office a few minutes ago," replied the pilot.

Quiñones walked to the office, lightly tapped on the door, and went inside.

The Chief Medical Flight Officer was facing away from the door, bent over a desk signing paperwork, when he entered. She stood straight upon hearing him, and said - "I just took a quick inventory of…"

"As did I," interrupted Quiñones, smirking as to his sexually suggestive comment.

The Chief Medical Flight Officer ignored him, and continued speaking. "I took a cursory inventory of how many medical supplies we have on board. This is going to take quite a while to audit, even with the assistance of DEA. My team needs to get on the move. What do you suggest?"

Quiñones became excited, recognizing that this situation worked to his advantage. He spoke quickly. "My suggestion is that you only send one doctor or nurse, up to you, and send the DEA quality folks with that individual. This eliminates overcrowding the aircraft, and allows them to do their chain of custody audits in flight, while not wasting precious time."

"No, that won't work," she replied. "What about the remainder of the medical staff? They are specialists that need to get to work the moment they touch down."

"They still can," replied Quiñones, not giving up on this opportunity. "I can get you another chopper, strictly for transporting personnel. It will not take much for me to arrange it, and they will arrive about ten to fifteen minutes behind the medical helo. How does that sound, Chief?" Quiñones smiled and winked at her.

"I suppose that I can live with ten to fifteen minutes lag time," she said, exasperated. "My most experienced doctor will accompany the DEA quality team. He can assist them with their audit."

Quiñones looked at his watch. "Let's get moving. I will make the necessary calls for your second chopper."

⌘⌘⌘

SEVEN

Now he that planteth and he that watereth are one: and every man shall receive his own reward according to his own labour - 1 Corinthians 3:8

Sharp, metallic sounds coupled with roars of fire filled the air, as the smoldering chopper plummeted to the ground. Upon impact, the helicopter expelled one final ball of fury in every direction. It was a scene reminiscent of a battle-hardened dragon, protesting its imminent death.

The explosion tossed Augustus several feet into the air. He crashed violently onto the frozen ground, and tumbled uncontrollably.

Augustus remained motionless upon his final somersault. He did not possess the strength necessary to move. His weakness did not stem from a physical limitation, but from a sheer lack of will.

Augustus sensed his spirit leave him. He breathed rapidly, thinking about all that had happened. He remained face down on the ground for what seemed to be an eternity. He then lifted his head, turned it, and rested his right cheek on the ground. He closed his eyes and saw images of his wife, Jennifer, holding their son, Nathaniel, during better times.

Tears streamed from Augustus' closed eyes as he whispered, "I failed the both of you. Please forgive me."

In an instant, the world around him fell silent.

෧෧෧

Trent Chism cursed as the storm intensified. He was upset not only at Mother Nature, but also at himself, for getting into this mess. The mighty engine that powered his oversized pickup truck struggled against the overbearing wind, whilst a barrage of sleet rendered his windshield wiper blades useless.

"I had no choice," he said aloud, banging the steering wheel with both hands, justifying his presence in this tempest. "I had to go. How could I have let that heifer give birth out in this storm? The calf would not have stood a chance."

Trent Chism was a cattle rancher unlike any other. Whereas the cattle trade traditionally resulted in the slaughter of animals for consumption, Trent's cattle never met such a fate.

CHISM'S CHAPERONES, the name of his ranch, raised cattle for the sole purpose of pairing them with organizations that catered to children with special needs. These mostly black and white cows provided education, and companionship, to "non neuro-typical" children in several dozen institutions across the country. It was a deeply fulfilling enterprise for Trent, which created a special bond between him and his cattle.

Due to this bond, Trent found himself deep within his five-hundred-acre ranch, moving one of his birthing heifers indoors. He did this to save her arriving calf from the storm he was currently battling.

After securely transporting the birthing heifer to a comfortable indoor shed, Trent pushed forward to get home, despite treacherous driving conditions.

As he focused on the path before him, he observed what appeared to be several headlights on his property. From what Trent could gather, there were two to three vehicles, about two hundred yards to his left. A moment later, Trent thought he was able to make out another set of vehicle lights. However, since the extra lights seemed much higher than the other ones, he dismissed it as some sort of reflection on his windshield due to the storm.

Prone to addressing unauthorized activity on his land, Trent instead decided to continue his trek home. "The storm most likely caused them to lose their way," he muttered. "I am not getting out in this mess to check on it. I will come back in the morning, once the storm passes, to look in on them, and find out what is going on."

Trent drove another ten minutes before reaching his house. As he drove up his driveway, he saw a ball of fire emerge in the sky off to his right. It was far enough away that he could not see exactly what it was. However, he could tell from the smoldering aspects of the fireball that some sort of explosion had occurred.

"Woah," he whispered, as he tried wiping condensation from the inside of his windshield with his jacket sleeve. "This is turning out to be one hell of a storm. I had better go see what that fire is all about."

The fireball Trent observed was a good distance from his land. Although he had opted not to stop, and check on the vehicles he believed to be lost on his property, he felt the need to go check on this.

"I am the only one who lives in a twenty-five-mile radius from here. If an aircraft went down, I am the only hope they have for survival. Those other folks have their vehicles, at least. They should be fine until daybreak."

The intensity of the storm let up slightly. Trent took advantage of the lull. He backed out of his driveway, and hurled his truck at top speed in the direction of the fireball.

꙳꙳꙳

Trent slowed his truck, and cautiously approached the burning wreckage. He could tell that an aircraft of some kind was engulfed in flames. However, he was unable to see, or otherwise determine, if anyone from that aircraft had survived.

Trent stopped driving. He wanted to avoid, at all costs, being the cause of a survivor's death by accidentally driving over them.

The glowing flames from the wreckage only partially illuminated the area around it. Trent turned on the flood lamps mounted atop his truck. It took no more than a few seconds for him to see the body.

Trent immediately jumped out of the truck, and ran to it.

The sleet had stopped falling, but the wind remained severe. For every step Trent took forward, the wind blew him back two.

I must reach that body, he thought. *The person might still be alive, and needing aid.*

To avoid further delay, Trent dropped onto his stomach. He did this to get aerodynamic. He then crawled to the body.

Trent finally reached it, and quickly checked for any signs of life.

꙳꙳꙳

The mental images of Jennifer and Nathaniel slowly gave way to empty, white space. Augustus was unable to hear, feel or see anything. He did not possess the mental wherewithal to understand what had happened to him.

Augustus was in a state of shock, and the concept of time did not resonate with him.

On the other side of this empty, white space was a time deep in Augustus' past. Although unable to grasp what was currently happening to him, Augustus did comprehend that the images he now saw were of his own memories.

It was the 1980's, and Augustus was in his hometown of New York City. This was a violent era throughout the city's five boroughs; a time where gritty lawlessness, and predatory gangs, ruled the streets.

Augustus was a young man during this period, and was not immune from the savagery. Fate had seen to it that he would find himself square in the middle of it all by the time he reached the age of 17.

The violence raged like a wildfire. Yet, the citizenry's grief-stricken cries fell silent upon politicians, the court system, and most law enforcement officials.

The Big Apple seemed to be poised for a catastrophic end. However, from this despair arose a mighty reaction.

A secret society comprised of NYC officials with personal ties to the city's wealthiest residents emerged. The group would convene in secrecy for the sole purpose of developing a solution to this crisis.

These officials, and their wealthy donors, favored a brutal response to the unspeakable atrocities being committed daily by unchecked criminals.

In the end, the group unanimously agreed that conventional policing methods would be futile. For civility to be restored, the chaos needed to be eradicated, and a clandestine solution was required.

What resulted was the creation of an unfathomable institution of killers whose task was to quell the violence.

Leading this institution, codenamed La Sombra Silenciosa (The Silent Shadow) was a man with vast experience in quashing insurgent uprisings throughout the globe. That man's name was C. Virgil Milken.

To accomplish their duty, these exterminators prowled the seedy New York City streets day and night, in all five boroughs, eliminating gang leaders, and those who profited from the violence. It was a merciless campaign of targeted executions.

At the time of La Sombra Silenciosa's creation, Augustus had been serving as an enforcer for one of New York City's most violent Chinese gangs.

It did not take long for Milken to learn of, and admire, Augustus' innate talents.

The mental image now presenting itself to Augustus was of the first time he met Milken. That memory was of an authoritative and convincing leader, who explained his need for Augustus to join the eradication campaign.

Various memories of their developing relationship zipped through Augustus' mind. The final memory was of the time that ultimately placed him on the path to the life he ended up living. It was the moment Milken asked him to take his talents to the world stage.

Augustus recalled genuine compassion coming from Milken in that moment, as he reached out with his right hand, while placing his left hand on Augustus' shoulder, saying - "Join me. Join us. We need you. Your country needs you. You will enlist in the United States Navy. Shortly thereafter, you will be rejected for a medical condition, but you will not be officially discharged. You will go off the grid, so to speak, and become a part of our global network. Come with me. Come with me..."

ൟൟൟ

Trent reached the body and searched for any obvious signs of injury.

He found none.

Next, he tapped the man lightly, to see if he would move.

Nothing happened.

Trent was about to place his ear down by the man's face, to listen for breathing.

Suddenly, the man moaned.

"Oh man, he's alive!" Trent exclaimed.

Trent quickly got up, and returned to his truck to grab a blanket and water.

The wind continued its relentless onslaught upon Trent. However, the adrenaline rushing through his veins appeared to make him impervious to the elements. He remained upright. The need to crawl seemingly disappeared.

Trent arrived at his truck, grabbed what he needed, and returned to the survivor.

Trent placed the blanket over the man, tucked in the edges, and nudged him on the shoulder, encouraging him to wake up.

Next, Trent opened a bottle of water, and poured some onto the man's lips, in a further effort to wake him.

The man continued to moan slightly, and babbled a few words, as if he were dreaming.

Trent nudged him several more times, saying - "Hey buddy, wake up. We need to get out of here. You need to wake up, and come with me. Come on; wake up. Let's get out of here. Come with me."

It did not work.

Trent reached to his side for the water bottle again. Upon straightening himself, he encountered a physical force, the type of which he had never experienced.

৵৵৵

Augustus was in and out of consciousness. In his stupor, he likened Trent's words to those he recalled Milken saying to him, during that life-altering moment.

Slowly emerging from his blurred state of mind, he recalled the current Hell that Milken imposed upon him, and his family.

Feeling a hand on his shoulder, Augustus associated that touch with Milken's.

He believed that he had the drop on this monster, and was prepared to end the atrocity.

৵৵৵

The vice-like grip on Trent's throat caused his vision to blur. His ears began to ring loudly. Trent was helpless. He let his arms fall to his sides as Augustus thrust him backwards onto the ground.

Augustus, trying to regain clarity of thought, shook his head wildly while maintaining his grip on Trent's throat. He looked around, and saw the burning chopper. He then peered down at Trent.

Augustus gasped upon realizing the moment he was in, and immediately released him.

Trent had already lost consciousness, due to the restriction of oxygen and blood to his brain.

Augustus checked Trent's pulse to determine if he killed him. "Gracias a Dios," said Augustus, thanking God. "I did not kill this man."

However, the pulse was very weak. Augustus quickly bent over, and administered CPR to revive him fully.

Upon awakening, Trent scurried backwards and away from Augustus in terror.

"No, don't worry," said Augustus, stretching his arms out towards Trent. "I did not mean to attack you. I was not coherent. I thought you were here to kill me. I am very sorry."

Trent touched his throat, and pointed towards the water.

Augustus handed the bottle to him.

Trent took a large gulp and said, "I suppose, if you wanted to kill me, you wouldn't have performed CPR to wake me up."

Augustus, in an attempt at offering some levity to the situation, replied - "Well, that is true, unless I was a sadistic maniac, and did not want you to die before I had the opportunity to torture the shit out of you."

Trent did not see the humor in that statement, and asked - "Who are you?"

"It does not matter who I am," replied Augustus. "What does matter is that we get out of here."

Augustus scanned the area saying, "They will be coming soon to make sure they got me."

"Woah, what?"

"Shut up!" Augustus shouted.

Trent ignored him, and kept asking questions. "Were you the pilot on that aircraft? Is there anyone else we should be looking for? How many people—"

Augustus cupped Trent's mouth with his hand. He then growled, "If you want to live, you must not speak, and you must listen to me. Do I make myself clear?"

Trent's eyes were wide. He nodded quickly in the affirmative.

Augustus eyed Trent up and down, and released him.

Trent immediately reached into his mouth.

Augustus gave him an inquisitive look.

"It felt like you squeezed the teeth off my jaw. You have one hell of a grip."

Augustus waved Trent towards his truck, saying - "Let's go. I will explain it to you on the way out."

ॐ ॐ ॐ

Augustus had no intentions of sharing explicit details of his dilemma with this man. Nevertheless, if he was not prepared to kill him, which he was not, then he had to tell him something credible.

Trent's intention was to drive Augustus as far away from his home as he could get. *There is no way I am taking this psycho back to my place,* he thought while listening to the story that Augustus was telling. *Yeah, right. Someone shot down the helicopter he was on in order to kill him.*

Trent glanced at Augustus as he continued to speak. Trent offered him a slight smile, and slowly nodded his head in acknowledgement of what he was hearing. He then turned his attention back to the road in front of him.

I would sooner believe him if he had told me that he tried to hijack the copter, but that the pilot made a kamikaze dive instead of giving up. I am taking his ass to the sheriff's department and let them deal with him.

However, Trent heard Augustus say something that caused a chill to run up and down his spine.

He slammed on the brakes.

The sudden stop, coupled with wet pavement, caused the truck to careen dangerously out of control.

Augustus had no idea what prompted this reaction from Trent, so he shouted - "What's the matter? What do you see? Is there someone following us?"

The truck safely came to a halt.

Trent wasted no time and began to speak. "Go back a little bit in your story. Like, right before I slammed on the brakes."

Augustus thought for a moment, then asked - "Um, the part about how I believe a drone shot down the chopper because—"

"No, no, a little bit before that. It was something about where you were going."

"Oh, right," recalled Augustus. "Well, I don't know if I talked about where I was going, per se. What I told you was that the pilot informed me he was taking me to the next leg of my journey."

"Okay," said Trent, hurriedly. "How far away from your next leg were you when you supposedly got shot down?"

"A few minutes at most, why?"

Trent told him of the vehicles he came across on his property several minutes prior to observing the fireball in the sky.

"That's them," said Augustus. "Take me to them."

"But they were trying to kill you. Why would you—?"

Augustus glared at him without saying a word.

Trent quit talking and took off to where he saw the intruders on his property.

"They would have killed you, you know, if you had stopped to question them," said Augustus. "Quite frankly, I'm surprised they didn't kill you before they went onto your field, so as to mitigate the risk of detection."

"My precious darlings prove their angelical powers yet again," said Trent.

"What's that?" Augustus asked.

Trent explained the business of his ranch, and of his being in the field most of the evening with a birthing heifer.

"They are waiting for you," said Augustus, sternly.

Trent looked at him.

"Your home," continued Augustus. "They most certainly went to your home to kill you earlier tonight. Not finding you there, they would have left someone to await your return. Your cows saved your life."

Trent cried, "Oh, my God. What am I going to do?"

"Reclaim your home," said Augustus. "How far are we?"

Trent gulped hard, and replied - "Just around the next bend, about three minutes away."

෨෨෨

The interior of the modestly sized ranch house was dark, and cool. On occasion, a metallic clunking sound reverberated throughout the home, followed by a minute-long hiss. These sounds represented the home's heating system kicking in. It was hardly enough warmth for most people to consider comfortable, making it apparent to the intruder lurking within that the occupant preferred an unusually chilled environment.

The intruder did not expect to remain in this house for as long as he had. He thought for sure the owner would have returned several hours ago. He observed the man leave during daylight hours, and assumed it was to work some chores on his land.

"I should have followed him, and killed him in the field," whispered the intruder. "That is what I get for wanting to provide him the dignity of dying in his own home."

The intruder went to the front porch window to look outside. Instantly, he dove to avoid a wash of light coming from a set of truck headlights outside. He quickly reached for his compact two-way radio to communicate the status to his leader, who was with the rest of the team in the fields beyond.

"Eggs are in the basket," he whispered into the radio.

"Scramble them up," replied the team leader.

The intruder clipped the radio to his belt, and prepared for his assault.

෨෨෨

Trent swore he was about to have a heart attack. His palms were clammy, and his mouth was desert dry. His vision blurred, due to hard and painful throbs of blood rushing through them.

Augustus had warned Trent that he must follow every detail of his plan.

"Success means that you live." These words from Augustus kept playing in Trent's mind over, and over, again.

Trent got ahold of himself, and focused on the remainder of what Augustus told him.

"Whoever is in your home will move swiftly. There may be more than one person inside, but it is highly unlikely given that you are not a professional killer. Let me worry about that detail. Your home is out in the middle of nowhere, where loud noises are of no concern to a marauder. Thus, the killer will undoubtedly use a gun, as opposed to something quieter, like a knife. The most important thing you must remember is this: Do not take more than one footstep into your house. If you do, I cannot help you, and you will die."

Trent took a deep breath, and strolled confidently to his front door.

He was to refrain from exhibiting cautiousness, or fear. His movements had to be convincing to anyone watching from inside that he suspected nothing.

Trent grabbed the handle to his front door and, without hesitation, opened it.

❧❧❧

Trent Chism was not a married man, and lived alone. Standing in the open doorway, he looked at the foyer area in front of him. It appeared to be tranquil. However, Trent sensed unusual energy all around him. His mind raced with many thoughts in the space of a nanosecond.

Am I truly picking up on a negative force from within my home, or am I spooked by what Augustus told me?

He had no way of knowing whether Augustus spoke the truth, or if he was crazy. Opting to err on the side of caution, Trent continued with the plan.

As Trent stepped inside, he simultaneously put his mobile phone up to his ear. The plan called for Trent to fake answering a telephone call at that precise moment.

"This is Trent," he said into the lifeless phone. He spoke quickly, and stopped walking.

"Oh, hi Sheriff, I was just– What's that? On my property, you say? No, I didn't see anyone in my fields. I've been out in them all day. Now, where exactly are they? I'll meet you there. I'm leaving now."

As instructed, Trent did not step further into his home. Instead, he spun around, shut the door behind him, and walked to his truck.

☙☙☙

The intruder waited anxiously as the home's occupant approached the front door. This anticipation thrilled the intruder, generating a smile upon his rugged face. He enjoyed nothing more than ambushing his prey. A moment like this was priceless to him.

His plan was to wait for the occupant to enter the home, and close the door, before launching his assault. A closed door precluded an immediate route for escape, should the first shot not kill the occupant.

The intruder held a .9mm handgun up by his chest with both hands. As the moment drew nearer, he lightly caressed the shaft of the weapon with his index finger. This routine helped ease the onslaught of excitement that always overcame him right before he attacked.

The door opened.

The intruder inhaled slowly, and deeply.

As the occupant entered, he started to speak.

The intruder took a quick glance around to see if someone had accompanied the occupant. He saw no one. The intruder then realized that the occupant was on a phone call.

He listened intently to what the occupant had to say. The intruder's eyes grew wide upon hearing the occupant's words.

Shit, he thought. *This is going to get messy fast. I must kill this man quickly, and then notify the team that law enforcement is heading towards them.*

The gleeful anticipation he had been enjoying ended abruptly. A depressive anticlimax replaced it when the occupant turned around and left.

The intruder wasted no time. He bolted forward towards the now closed front door, hurtling a sofa in the process. He moved so fast, he crashed into the door as he grabbed its knob. He then yanked it open, and charged outside to pursue the occupant.

ৡৡৡ

Trent vomited from fear upon hearing movement inside his home.

"It was true," he whispered, as a tear rolled down his cheek. "There really is someone in my house that wants to kill me."

He then heard what sounded like a crash, followed by the sound of his front door opening forcefully.

Trent tried to continue walking, but he froze. "Please don't kill me," he said, softly.

A thick, harsh voice boomed at him from behind. "Who else besides the Sheriff is headed to confront my team?"

Trent, almost by reflex, raised his hands into the air, and turned to face this menace. He was about to plead for his life when he saw blood spurt outward from the man's collarbone area.

The intruder instinctively spun, raising his weapon, and reaching to touch his wound. But the shot that just went through him was devastating, and he plummeted to the ground without firing back.

Augustus walked to the mortally wounded man, and looked at the gun he just used to blast him from the rear. He then said to Trent, "You know, these old Colt .45 revolvers are great, but I could never really aim that well with them."

Trent looked at Augustus with horror.

Augustus kneeled by the writhing man, and continued speaking to Trent. "I was aiming a bit lower, in between the shoulder blades. Now, I don't think he is useful to me."

Augustus then spoke to the intruder. "Can you talk?"

The intruder grabbed onto Augustus' arm, and shook it violently. His eyes rolled back into his head as he struggled to breathe.

"No, you cannot," said Augustus, answering for the intruder.

Trent, now standing alongside of them, said - "I've had that gun for years. I kept it in my truck in the event I needed to scare off coyotes and other predators. I never shot into something alive, and never at a person."

"Well, this here is not the type of predator you can scare away with a shot," said Augustus. "This is one that you have to kill."

He then pulled a knife from his boot, and slammed it into the intruder's chest, striking his heart, and killing him instantly.

"Why did you have to use a knife?" Trent shouted, mortified at the brutality of this method of killing.

"His friends are nearby," replied Augustus. "If they hear one shot, they will assume it was the one that killed you. If they hear a second one, it will create curiosity, and put them on alert. We don't want that."

"Can you please just tell me who you really are, and what you do, exactly?" Trent pleaded.

Augustus replied, "I am a simple public servant. Now, take me to where you saw the others."

❧❧❧

Trent had no choice but to come to terms with all that was happening. A thought came to him as he observed Augustus pull the knife from the dead man's chest.

"More weapons," said Trent.

"What did you say?" Augustus asked.

"You need more weapons than what you currently have on your person," replied Trent.

"Well, is there a gun store around here that I can pillage?" Augustus mocked, knowing that they were in the middle of nowhere.

Trent smiled and said, "Come with me."

He led Augustus to a small, brick structure attached to the rear of his house. He then entered a passcode into the security pad that protected it from unauthorized entry.

Augustus surveyed the structure with a curious eye, and said - "I am intrigued by the possibilities of what is inside this building."

"Not much of a building, really," replied Trent. "I think of it as an oversized storage unit."

"Yeah, that is protected well, with no windows," observed Augustus.

Trent opened the heavy metal door, and flicked on the lights.

"Come on in," Trent said with a large grin.

Along each wall were eight rows stocked neatly with various weapons. There were handguns, shotguns, and semi-automatic rifles of different calibers. There was also enough ammunition to invade a small country.

Augustus was stunned upon seeing a crate on the floor that contained what appeared to be hand grenades.

"What in the world?" Augustus exclaimed.

"Let me explain," said Trent. "You don't get to live way out in these parts without being into firearms. Me, I am not a gun enthusiast. In fact, I hate them. They scare the heck out of me. But what scares me more are the whacko zealots that inhabit this area who judge everyone based on their stance on gun ownership rights. You know, Second Amendment kind of crap. Anyhow, since the locals already view me strangely for raising cattle I will not slaughter, I thought it best to show up at every gun show in the area, and buy as much high-powered weaponry I could afford. My strategy is simple. I make my appearance, talk about shooting things into oblivion, and walk out of the show armed to the teeth."

Dumbfounded, Augustus simply replied, "That makes sense." He then pointed to the crate on the floor with the grenades, and asked, "Do they sell those at gun shows here?"

"Oh, heck no," replied Trent. "That came from some nut job who took one hell of a liking to me due to all of the weapons and ammo I've bought over time. Yeah, that guy, he really is something else. He gets all kinds of explosives from the black market. He tells me he was some sort of Army Special Forces soldier in the past. I think he said he was a Ranger, or something like that. Who knows, either way, the guy gets his hands on a lot of stuff, and seems to really know his way around weapons."

Augustus looked to the floor, fixated on what Trent just said and whispered, "Yeah, I know a former Army Special Forces guy. He is one hell of a man, and is prepared to give his life for me, and my family, even as we speak."

Augustus moved further into the armory, started grabbing items, and said, "We need to get this done, right now."

⌘⌘⌘

EIGHT

Hoc voluerunt (They wished this) - Julius Caesar, after defeating Pompey in the battle of Pharsalus

Quiñones hung up the telephone, and said to the Chief Medical Flight Officer, "I have it all arranged. The personnel chopper will be here in about twenty minutes. Sorry, that is as quick as I could muster one up."

She frowned, and replied, "It is not an optimal plan, and I am not happy about it. However, given the circumstances, it will have to do."

"I appreciate your willingness to cooperate," he replied. "I will notify the DEA team that they are to depart at once."

He then exited her office.

అ అ అ

Quiñones hustled to the NICO Aardvarks posing as DEA personnel. Wasting no time, he briefed them on the plan to get them onto the chopper.

The team nodded in acknowledgement.

The Chief Medical Flight Officer appeared, and said, "This is Doctor Douglas Benson. He will accompany you on this flight."

The Aardvarks dismissively nodded, and greeted the doctor with barely audible grunts.

"Great, let's get going then, shall we?" said Quiñones, hurriedly.

"No, not so fast," said Milagros, the female Aardvark.

Quiñones, visibly disturbed, feared what would come out of her mouth next.

"As I understand it," said Milagros, "we are going into a potentially hostile area. My team and I are unarmed, as you can see. Although we are DEA quality control personnel, we have all qualified with weapons at the Federal Law Enforcement Training Center. We need weapons."

Quiñones was dumbfounded, and did not know what to say. However, the Chief Medical Flight Officer presented a solution.

"An advance team is on the ground with the protected parties. Although they are already heavily armed, there are crates of weapons, and other supplies, that we will deliver to them later today. I suppose you and your team can pick what you like, and leave those weapons with them upon your return. How does that sound?"

"Your words are about as beautiful as you are," replied Milagros.

The Chief Medical Flight Officer smiled at her and said, "There is a cantina just off base that I'll be having some drinks at this evening, if you would like to join me."

Milagros smiled, and replied, "I can taste the margarita on my lips already."

Quiñones scratched his head as he listened to their conversation and thought, *That is not who I had hoped would be sleeping with the Chief tonight...ugh...*

❧❧❧

The droning sounds of the medical helicopter coming to life filled the air as the Aardvarks chose their weapons from the crates. After getting what they needed, they stood in a straight line, waiting for the pilot's signal to board.

The pilot, after determining that the rotor RPMs reached one hundred percent, waved everyone onboard.

The group quickly entered the chopper.

Once everyone settled in, the doctor slid the chopper door shut, and sat down.

A male Aardvark, named Trask, gave the doctor a once over, taking notice of the nametag on his flight suit. The tag did not contain the doctor's name. Rather, it had what appeared to be a nickname.

"Stitch? I thought she said your name is Douglas Benson," queried Trask.

"Doctor Douglas Benson, to be exact," he replied. "Stitch is a nickname I received while serving in the Navy. It is my call sign now."

Trask could not help but mock the doctor. "Is that so? How did you get that nickname, Stitch? Did you have to patch up papercut wounds for your fellow squids?"

"I did have to patch up my fellow squids, as you call them, but for injuries much more serious than papercuts. To be fair, I had to patch up plenty of Army, Marine, and Air Force personnel, too."

"Oh man, this doc is a trip," Trask said to his team. "I think we have ourselves some in-flight entertainment."

The Aardvarks roared with laughter.

Trask continued with his sarcastic line of questioning.

"So, you get a nickname that morphs into a call sign just because you've sewn up a few grunts, jarheads, squids, and fly-boys? That is something else, Jack, I tell you what."

"Quit fucking with him, and let's get with it," said Milagros.

"No, that's fine," Stitch said to her. "I can take it." He then addressed the team:

"I spent a dozen years serving as a Combined Reconnaissance Team (CRT) combat surgeon. A P.J., which stands for Parachute Jumper, if you are not familiar with the reference. I was trained to HALO jump into firefights whenever special forces dialed 911. I am also trained to perform surgery aboard helicopters. The funny thing, though, is that I caused more casualties than what I saved. I did more fighting than healing. Hence, the nickname Stitch. If you came across my path, your odds of needing stitches as a result of that contact were much higher than having your ass medically stabilized by me."

Stitch sensed a strange energy emit from this crew of DEA quality control personnel. He could not put a finger on it, but he felt uneasy. Something about the way they carried themselves; the way they moved. Nothing about this group was consistent with what one would expect from a unit of inventory control specialists.

This crew looks more like a team of government security contractors than anything else, he thought.

Stitch decided not to pursue his instincts. Instead, he would simply keep an eye on them, while treading lightly around their large egos.

"I am hopping off the moment we touch down," said Stitch. "My understanding is that a young child and his mother need immediate medical attention."

The Aardvarks eyed each other without saying a word.

"You do what you have to, doc," said Milagros. "We will focus on completing what we came here to do as well."

"Shouldn't you be taking inventory of the drugs prior to us landing?" Stitch asked, unable to refrain from prying.

"Look, candy stripe," shouted Trask. "Don't you go worrying your pretty little squid ass about us getting our job done. We have it handled. You just focus on being a good nurse."

Laughter erupted within the helicopter.

Stitch feigned amusement by the words as well, and joined them. However, he became more troubled. During the raucous laughter, Stitch observed Milagros whisper into the ear of a team member, who simultaneously glanced at Stitch while nodding.

"Three minutes to touchdown," the pilot shouted back to them.

"Has the other helo taken off yet?" asked Milagros.

"Negative ma'am, she should be airborne in fifteen minutes."

"That is all the time we need," she replied, speaking more to the Aardvarks than to the pilot.

All the time we need for what? That is the question, thought Stitch. He then swung his medical backpack over his shoulders, and prepared himself for whatever was to come.

THUMP, THUMP, THUMP, THUMP, THUMP...

ॐॐॐ

The BOPS advance team, charged with the duty of protecting Augustus' family, as well as the Bakers, hustled about the property.

"Bird inbound sir," shouted a BOPS agent to his commander.

"Have we verified that they are friendly?" queried the commander.

"Negative, sir," replied the agent. "Comms are somewhat sporadic out here. I can't hail the pilot over the net."

"Establish an iron ring," the commander ordered. "Kill anyone that does not comply with our orders upon exiting the craft."

A collective response of, "Roger that, sir!" followed the directive.

Doctor Broderson approached the commander, and asked, "Shall I wait here with you, so that I can escort the medical personnel to the patients? Or do you prefer that I standby elsewhere?"

"Nah, stay put," the commander replied. "I ordered the team to set up a tight perimeter, an iron ring, as a precautionary measure. Besides, it would be nearly impossible for a threat to be on board that chopper. We run a near perfect operation wherever we go, from A to Z, you can count on that."

"Please pardon my ignorance, but what is an iron ring?" Broderson queried.

"There is no need to apologize, doctor," replied the commander. "My shooters are positioned in a half-circle formation, covering one hundred eighty degrees around the chopper's landing zone. Nothing hostile can survive that level of overwatch."

"What about the rest of the circle?" Broderson asked. "A one hundred eighty-degree perimeter leaves open another one hundred eighty degrees, does it not? It sounds more like a half iron ring…or am I missing something?"

The commander snorted, and replied, "To an untrained eye, it would seem to be lacking. Nevertheless, that is all the terrain my men need to cover in order to suppress an unlikely attack. We've got this, doctor."

"I mean no disrespect, commander. However, after everything I have experienced these past several weeks, I have grown skeptical of infallible plans. I think I will observe from inside the front door," said Broderson.

"As you wish, doctor," chuckled the commander.

∽∽∽

The medical helicopter circled the compound, searching for a suitable landing zone.

On the ground, two BOPS agents waved marshalling wands, signaling it to land at their position.

The pilot aggressively angled the helo towards them, and swiftly landed the aircraft.

Stitch slid open the helicopter's door as it descended, ready to hit the ground running. He sat on the edge of the floor, dangling his legs outside the aircraft, his feet barely above the skids.

"Touchdown in five, four, three, two, one," announced the pilot, via the craft's speaker system.

Upon landing, Stitch leapt off the chopper. Just as he jumped, a metallic sound from within the craft caught his attention. Curious, he turned his head in the direction of the sound. What he saw appalled him.

The metallic sound was of Milagros chambering a round into her weapon.

Stitch observed Milagros shoot the pilot in the head at pointblank range.

Stunned, Stitch twisted in the air uncontrollably, causing him to hit the ground awkwardly, and hard. Lying on his back, he saw Milagros turn her attention from the dead pilot, to him.

Milagros positioned herself at the helicopter doorway, and pointed her weapon directly at Stitch.

Stitch had no weapon to defend himself. Moreover, the medical backpack he wore was at maximum capacity with supplies, and was extremely heavy. He had as much mobility as a turtle on its back.

Stupefied, Stitch looked at Milagros as she winked, and smiled at him.

"Oh, shit," he said.

҈ ҈ ҈

Doctor Broderson anxiously awaited the chopper's arrival from within the building's main entrance. The aircraft not only brought much needed supplies, and medical personnel, but it also served as his extraction from this dreadful experience.

Although he had developed a strong bond with Jennifer, Augustus' wife, and their son Nathaniel, this experience was much more than what he anticipated. It also took him well past his emotional capacity.

"I am not built for this kind of chaos," he said, watching the chopper approach the landing zone. "I have done all that I can. I pray that I have saved at least one life throughout this fiasco."

Broderson looked back towards where Jennifer and Nathaniel were under guard by the Bakers. "I will miss both of you. I don't think that I will ever know where you end up. But if I do, I promise to check in on you."

He then looked back to the now descending helicopter.

"You ready, doc?" Cal asked, approaching him from behind.

"I am, Cal," replied Broderson. "I really am."

"On behalf of Augustus, doctor, thank you for all that you have done. His family would not be alive today had you not provided your assistance, and expertise. You are a remarkable man."

"I am honored that you feel that way," replied Broderson, "given the truly exceptional…that…your family…"

Broderson became distracted, and garbled his words upon hearing what sounded like gunfire come from the chopper.

Cal did not hesitate. He bolted to the helicopter. As he ran, he swung the rifle from over his shoulder, and held it in a shooting position.

Doctor Broderson heard Cal yelling, but he could not make out the words.

Broderson felt a rush of fear overcome him. He slowly ran an open palm across his face, and said - "Oh, my God. Please, not again."

ಶ್ಶಶ್ಶಶ್ಶ

Cal ran at full speed to the chopper, yelling at the BOPS agents stationed along the perimeter.

"Who is shooting? Are any of you shot? What the hell is going on?"

The agents heard the shot, but they failed to react.

Cal could not discern whether their immobilization was due to disbelief, confusion, or incompetence. He did not stop running to find out. Rather, he opted to engage this menace.

As he closed in, he saw a woman appear in the chopper's doorway. Next, he observed her point her weapon towards a man sprawled on the ground.

Cal did not know him, but the man was in the woman's sights, in real trouble, and in desperate need of assistance.

Nor did Cal know the woman. However, one of these two was an aggressor that undoubtedly had a devilish intention of harming the Peña family. But which one was it?

Cal saw evil in the woman's eyes as she prepared to kill the unarmed man on the ground.

"It's her," Cal said aloud. "She is here to kill the Peña family!"

Cal had no time to aim his weapon at the woman. Instead, he unleashed a barrage of shots towards the helicopter.

The woman escaped the volley by diving back inside the aircraft.

Stitch did not hesitate, and jumped into action. He quickly removed the medical backpack, and bolted towards Cal.

"I'm a doctor!" he yelled. "I don't know who they are," he said, pointing to the helicopter.

At that moment, two men with semiautomatic rifles appeared at the helicopter door, spraying bullets of their own.

Cal grabbed ahold of Stitch, and shouted, "Incoming, dive!"

Both men rolled over each other, as the return fire from the assassins sought their targets. Dirt, rocks, and soil spit up all around them, with rounds coming within an inch of their bodies.

A BOPS agent, stationed in the vicinity to where Cal and Stitch rolled, returned fire at the two assassins. He placed well-aimed shots at the invaders in rapid succession. One of those rounds struck an Aardvark's weapon, sending it through the air.

Furious over the shot that tore the weapon from his hands, the Aardvark, named Lucan, pounded his chest like a beast. It was at this point that he noticed his injuries. The force of the weapon being stripped from his two-handed grip had shredded his flesh.

Lucan looked wild-eyed at his wounds. Determined to continue the fight, he did not let the mangled flesh deter him. Years of ruthlessness had conditioned this man to improvise, and to complete his missions.

Lucan howled like a wild animal as he jumped off the chopper. His eyes were filled with rage. Fueled with an insatiable desire to kill, he lunged towards the BOPS agent that shot at him.

The agent, too, had many years of experience. However, he had never witnessed this level of combat. Consequently, the fury emanating from Lucan startled the agent, causing him to hesitate before deciding to shoot again.

This hesitation was all that Lucan needed.

Lucan leapt a distance equal to any lion in the wild, and pounced on the agent with merciless violence. This deranged Aardvark slashed, stabbed, and used his teeth to rip flesh off the screaming agent.

As this occurred, the other BOPS agents attempted to fight off the rest of the marauders. However, their efforts were short-lived.

The Aardvarks made short work of the BOPS agents defending the landing zone. With laser precision, the Aardvarks picked off each of the BOPS agents within a matter of seconds, including their commander, who had just moments ago assured of the landing zone's impenetrable security.

Blood from the slaughtered BOPS agent dripped from Lucan's mouth. He looked all around, searching for his next victim. Upon seeing Cal and Stitch, he roared like a mythical beast, and sprung towards them.

Cal steadied himself, and shot the approaching lunatic three times.

However, bullets appeared to have no effect on the raging maniac.

Cal pulled a tactical knife from his belt. He crouched slightly, and readied himself for hand-to-hand combat.

Just as Lucan closed in, Stitch tackled him from the side, slowing his momentum.

Simultaneously, Cal piled on top of them, seeking an opportunity to land a fatal blow with his knife upon this seemingly unstoppable creature.

ॐॐॐ

The three men screamed, scowled, and shouted obscenities, attempting to win this battle to the death.

Cal frantically probed Lucan's body for a vulnerable spot to exploit.

But Lucan wore extraordinary body armor, offering little to no opportunities, other than his sternum area.

Upon observing a tiny separation of material along that area, Cal thrust his knife towards it.

However, Lucan evaded the blow with a powerful spin, tossing Stitch in the process.

Returning to his feet, Stitch observed Cal attempt another strike at Lucan's sternum area.

Noticing the vulnerable spot that had attracted Cal's attention, Stitch jumped back into the fight. As he closed in on the battling duo, he dove, completed a forward roll and came to a full stop on the ground behind Lucan.

Situated in a sitting position, Stitch stretched both his legs forward, placing them between Lucan's legs. He then sprung onto his knees, causing his legs to interlock with Lucan's.

Stitch outstretched his arms upwards, positioning them underneath Lucan's armpits. Clamping his hands upon Lucan's shoulders, while holding on for dear life, Stitch allowed his deadweight to free fall backwards to the ground.

In a swift and calculated manner, Stitch wrapped his arms over Lucan's arms as they fell.

Upon hitting the ground, Stitch had total control over Lucan's mobility…for about three seconds.

As they dropped, Stitch screamed – "Get him now!"

Lucan roared like a trapped grizzly, as Stitch latched onto his limbs.

Without missing a beat, Cal dove onto the duo. He crashed into them with great force, almost knocking the wind out of himself.

Cal gripped his knife as tightly as he had ever held one in his life, and plunged the dagger into Lucan's sternum.

Blood spewed from Lucan's mouth, covering Cal's face and nearly blinding him. However, Cal did not need to see in order to get this done. He had killed many people in the name of duty, and knew how to do it well.

Cal sensed Lucan's life slowly fading away, but time was not to be wasted. It needed to happen right now, at this very moment.

The lives of Augustus's family were in imminent danger, and he needed to get by their side immediately.

Cal's grip began to slip, as blood covered the handle. He yelled fiercely, and gripped the knife tighter, causing pain to shoot up his arms.

Blinded by Lucan's blood, and his own tears from the pain, Cal propelled himself forward with one final surge of energy, twisting the dagger simultaneously.

Lucan's body spasmed violently.

His seizures caused Stitch to bang the back of his head several times on the ground, disorienting him.

Cal breathed heavily as he waited to confirm this maniac's death. Upon feeling the man's life pass, Cal rolled off, and onto his back.

"Oh, my God," he said, wiping blood, and tears from his face. "Are you alive under there?" He asked Stitch.

"Barely, but yeah," replied Stitch.

"How many more are there?" Cal asked.

"Seven in total, from what I could tell."

"I hate to play and run, but I have a family to protect. Those bastards killed our entire security detail," shouted Cal.

Cal stiffened with fear after saying these words. He came to the realization that, after killing the entire BOPS detachment, the attackers would have gone inside for their primary targets.

Distraught for having spent precious time battling this behemoth he just killed, instead of defending Augustus' family, Cal said, "I am so sorry, hermano. I have failed you. I deserve whatever wrath you wreak upon me for my ineffectiveness."

The area was now quiet. There were no sounds of struggle, or movement of any kind.

Stitch got out from under Lucan's corpse, and said, "I don't hear them out here. They must have gone to kill the family."

"I have no choice but to go back in there. I owe Augustus at least that much." Cal replied.

"Who is Augustus?" Stitch asked.

"Come with me, and I'll tell you –"

⌘⌘⌘

NINE

Doctor Broderson watched in horror as Cal, and another man, battled against an attacker.

Broderson felt faint. He wished that he could blend in with the trees, and avoid the conflict.

However, his near-crippling fear subsided upon witnessing the attackers methodically kill the BOPS agents. Somehow, this gruesome sight empowered him, and he felt mightier than he ever thought possible.

Broderson bolted to the Peña family, and arrived by their side moments later.

Papi, Cal's father, was with them.

Standing alongside him was a stocky, longhaired BOPS agent named Haaris.

Nearly hyperventilating, Broderson shouted, "The defense plan did not work! We must switch to the last resort plan that Cal devised!"

"Where is my Caleb?" Papi growled.

"I believe he is not going to make it. Mister Baker, we have no time. We must move the Peña family right now," Broderson pleaded.

Papi looked at Haaris, and nodded.

Haaris proceeded to prepare Jennifer and Nathaniel for relocation to the lowest level of the building.

Nathaniel was quietly sitting in a chair, holding onto a stuffed animal, looking at his mother Jennifer, who was laid out on a gurney. Moving her was going to take longer than it would with Nathaniel.

"We need a few more minutes," shouted Papi. "Once the Peña's are secure, I will execute the plan. Bo, get your butt out there, and buy this family more time. Every second counts, GO SON, GO!"

"I'm going, Pa!" Bo, Cal's brother, replied, as he turned to leave.

Doctor Broderson intended on accompanying Bo, to assist in any way possible. However, fate finally intervened…

&&&

The Aardvarks moved silently across the main level of the building. Each room contained antique furnishings, such as fine leather chairs, curtains made of lace, and diamond-encrusted chandeliers hanging from high above. It was apparent to these killers that the place was typically used for large, elitist gatherings.

But on this day, there would be no gala. There were no important hands to shake, or asses to kiss. The only thing for these killers to do here was to assassinate a mother, and her child.

"This is Flea," whispered the lead Aardvark into his microphone. "I am in the cocoon, and hear some movement in the next room."

The Aardvark behind him, Ty, whispered, "Yeah, I'm picking up movement from up ahead as well. We're going in."

"We're covering the main entrance," replied Milagros. "Chet is getting himself settled into the pilot's seat for exfiltration. Get it done, now."

"Roger that," replied Flea.

Although it was daylight outside, the interior of the building was extremely dark.

The two killers were thankful that they grabbed night vision goggles from the crates back at Apache South. The darkness of the interior created a need for them, and they slowly placed the goggles over their eyes.

Creeping with leopard-like grace as they approached their prey, they arrived at the room from which they heard movement.

"Bingo," said Flea, seeing the mother, child and three other people.

&&&

As instructed, Bo exited the room, but stopped suddenly as if he hit a wall.

In the darkness beyond, he saw what looked like two pair of giant insect eyes looking at him. He also saw the weapons that these curious figures were holding.

At first, Bo believed they were members of the BOPS detachment. However, when he saw them raise their weapons as if they were aiming, and ready to shoot at Jennifer, he knew they were here to kill.

Bo dove back towards the room, to block the shooters from hitting her.

"NO!!!" Bo yelled, as he went airborne to become her human shield.

Flea took the first shot, which landed squarely on Bo's left shoulder.

The bullet went clean through Bo, smashing into the rear wall of the room.

Haaris scooped up Nathaniel, and rolled across the floor with the child tucked in his arms, escaping harm.

Papi did not flinch, and unholstered his .357 revolver. He aimed, and said, "You sons of bitches have this coming."

The roar of the magnum Papi fired reverberated throughout the structure.

Flea felt the bullet's heat as it whizzed past his left ear.

Ty was not as fortunate. The magnum slug, finding its target on his forehead, blew his brains out as it exited.

Bo's shoulder sizzled from the bullet wound. But he could not be deterred. He rushed at Flea.

However, Flea was able to get off one more shot before Bo could reach him.

The bullet from Flea's weapon slammed into Jennifer's chest as she lay on the gurney, mortally wounding her.

As if in slow motion, Bo saw Jennifer's arm drop along the side of the gurney as blood trickled down it, dripping onto the floor from her fingertips.

Bo lunged at Flea, and grabbed him. He then picked the now screaming Flea up over his head, and body-slammed the assassin over a stair railing, breaking his back, and killing him.

Doctor Broderson dove into a different room, to avoid being pummeled by mistake.

Milagros, upon hearing the commotion inside, ran to offer backup to her comrades. But she arrived too late to save them.

Upon witnessing Flea's demise, Milagros raised her weapon, and shot at the man that just killed him.

Blood sprayed into the air as the bullet from Milagros' weapon hit Bo's upper body.

Bo fell to the floor. Although in pain, he managed to quickly scurry forward. He then wrapped his massive arms around the legs of the attacker who shot him.

Bo struck Milagros once in the face, but stopped punching upon realizing his attacker was a woman.

Unable to knowingly strike a woman due to his upbringing, Bo grabbed Milagros by her shirt, stood up, and tossed her like a bag of groceries.

"Go, get out of here!" he yelled at her.

Milagros rose to her feet, aimed her weapon at Bo, and pulled the trigger.

Her weapon did not fire. It jammed.

Bo, wild-eyed and amazed, took a step towards her.

Milagros did a roundhouse kick, her foot landing squarely against Bo's head.

Bo fell hard.

Milagros looked at her weapon, then down at Bo, and said, "You pussy."

She then fled in the direction from which she came.

Bo got up, wobbled briefly, and ran after her.

❧❧❧

As Cal and Stitch made their way to the Peña's, Bo appeared at the building's entrance.

Bo was shirtless, and his chest was full of blood.

Cal observed that Bo was chasing the woman from the chopper.

Behind Bo, and gaining momentum, were two assailants.

"Oh, no, Bo –" exclaimed Cal, expecting to witness the murder of his brother. "No! Bo!"

Cal charged to his brother's defense.

Stitch followed close behind.

Cal hollered as he dashed through the brush, to distract Bo's pursuers. He then squeezed off several shots at the attacker closest to Bo.

The rounds struck their target. However, they had minimal effect against the state-of-the-art protective gear the assailants wore.

POP, POP, POP…three shots from an assailant's weapon found their mark, striking Bo.

Cal yelled an impossible scream, and ran even faster to his brother.

His uptick in speed created more distance between him and Stitch. Without warning, Milagros occupied the space between them.

"You are not getting away from me again, pendejo," she said, aiming her weapon at Stitch. She then pulled the trigger, twice.

THUD, THUD…the sounds of bullets smashing into flesh owned that moment in time.

ৰৈৰৈৰৈ

Doctor Broderson cautiously made his way out from the room he dove into for cover. He looked around, and saw no one.

Broderson became overwhelmed with a strong intuition.

"I need to check on Cal. He may be dying alone out there. The least I can do is offer him some comfort," he uttered.

Upon exiting the building, he observed Bo running wildly, with attackers in pursuit.

"He is luring them to the traps Cal set," Broderson said. "God, I hope he makes it."

He then caught sight of Cal. It was a blessed sight. Cal was alive! However, it appeared that Cal was about to engage in an act of violence, in defense of his brother.

Broderson also saw the man who fought alongside Cal earlier by the chopper. He was trying to keep up with Cal, ostensibly to assist him again.

But Broderson noticed a danger lurking in the woods, which was closing in on that young man, fast.

It was Milagros, and she was stalking Stitch.

It appeared to Broderson that Milagros was about to pounce on Stitch.

Broderson tapped a speed within him he never knew existed, and lunged onto Milagros as she prepared to fire her weapon.

The two blasts from her gun deafened Broderson.

᪥᪥᪥

Stitch fell to the ground, landing on a large, protruding rock. He felt numb across his chest, shoulders, and arms.

The chaotic noise around him ceased, leaving behind an eerie silence.

Stitch tried to get up, but his arms were too weak. Years of combat experience as a CRT surgeon had prepared him for many situations, but not for this. Nothing about his current predicament made any sense. His only thought was, if he lived, he needed to make a greater contribution to this world.

Stitch managed to get onto his feet.

Sensation in his chest, shoulders, and arms slowly returned. He rubbed his upper body, and realized that the rock he smacked into is what caused his numbness, not bullets.

"I thought for sure she shot me," he said.

He took several steps, and stopped by a dying man.

Stitch knelt beside the man. He read aloud the nametag on the man's lab coat, as he gasped his final breaths, "Doctor Broderson."

᪥᪥᪥

Doctor Broderson let out a high pitch squeal of pain, as the bullets made their way through his body.

But the pain was short-lived, with a sense of peace and tranquility replacing it.

His life's most joyous moments appeared before his eyes.

A vision of his mother, who had long since passed away, manifested alongside of him.

With great agony, Doctor Broderson reached for his mother's arm, to hold her. He then spoke to her, and said in his final breaths, "You will be proud of me, mother. I saved a life today."

ೲೲೲ

As he had numerous times throughout his career, Stitch administered last rites.

The doctor said something barely audible to Stitch, and perished.

Stitch closed the doctor's eyelids, and stood up.

He stepped around the doctor's body, and knelt by the other corpse.

"Isn't that some crazy luck?" Stich said.

Stitch analyzed the female corpse, by examining the entry wound, located under her chin.

Next, he examined an entry wound, and an exit wound, on the doctor.

Speaking to the dead woman, Stitch said, "It looks like this one bullet ricocheted through the good doctor, after you shot him at close range. It then found its way into your skull after exiting his body. This is the greatest example of poetic justice, plain and simple."

Stitch rose to his feet, and scanned the area to locate Cal.

Neither Cal, nor his brother, were in the vicinity.

Stitch walked towards the last spot he saw them. He needed to know if they were either dead or wounded.

Stitch abruptly stopped walking.

A *SWOOSH* sound filled the air, followed by a large, hot wind…and an enormous ball of fire.

"What now?" Stitch shouted, diving onto the ground to avoid incineration.

⌘⌘⌘

TEN

"**B**o, we need to get out of here!" Cal shouted, as he approached his wounded brother.

Bo was lying on his stomach, trying to get to his feet.

Cal had managed to divert the two attackers pursuing Bo, by tossing a couple of shock grenades at them.

"They will not be spooked for long," Cal said. "Get moving, or we will die right here in this spot."

With help from his brother, Bo stood up.

The two injured brothers staggered to a thick row of trees, located along the rear of the building.

"Where are they, Caleb?" Bo asked, concerned with the whereabouts of the attackers.

"I saw them retreat to their chopper. They are probably there to regroup, and will undoubtedly push back hard on us," replied Cal.

"Caleb," said Bo. "They killed her…Nate's momma is dead, and THEY killed her. Pa shot one of the killers in the head, and I killed the other one by breaking his back."

"You and Pa did exactly what you needed to do," Cal said, wiping away tears after hearing of Jennifer's death.

"I don't think they got Nate," said Bo. He then asked, "Do you think Pa is with Nate?"

"If Nate is still alive, I am confident that Pa is with him. And, I'll tell you something else, brother. I am pretty damn sure that Pa is about to put my last resort plan into motion, so we better get to cover fast!"

঱঱঱

Trask, and another Aardvark named Hatch, retreated to the chopper.

Hatch jumped inside. He returned shortly with a large quantity of ammunition.

"We need to make our final push on these pricks, and get the fuck out of here," Hatch said, as he handed ammo to Trask.

"There's only three of us left," Trask grunted. "Those lucky-assed weekend warriors need to be snuffed out, pronto."

The operative who intended on piloting the Aardvarks out of this mess, named Chet, appeared at the helicopter's doorway.

Chet only took part in the initial assault upon the chopper's touchdown. He then remained behind to guard the aircraft, and to settle himself into the piloting position for the team's exfiltration once they completed their mission. Consequently, he was unaware of what occurred beyond the landing zone.

"What is the status on the family?" Chet asked.

"I can't say for sure," replied Trask.

"We know that Flea believed he had found them, based on his last communication. But he's dead, along with Ty," Hatch said, "So we cannot confirm that the family is dead. Their security detail is defending the structure solidly. I can only assume that the family is still alive in there, somewhere."

"What exactly do you mean by defending the structure solidly?" Chet asked.

Hatch replied, "Well, breaching the structure was not much of an issue. The front door was wide open. Flea and Ty entered first, probing the West wing of the structure. Trask and I worked our way across the East wing."

"What sort of resistance did you encounter?" Chet asked.

"Zero," replied Hatch.

"That doesn't sound like a solid defense to me, zit face," Chet said, angrily.

Hatch ignored the commentary, and continued with his narrative. "We found a stairwell to the lower level. We intended on going downstairs, to look for the family. However, upon hearing Flea's communication about possibly locating the family, we broke towards his vector."

"And?" Chet asked, impatiently.

"All Hell broke loose from there," interjected Trask.

"It sure did," Hatch agreed.

"There was a loud yell, followed by a crashing sound. There was more yelling, and what sounded like a cannon being shot off," Trask said. "We then double-timed to get to Flea and Ty, but when we got to the entryway area, we saw Milagros running out with some gorilla of a man chasing her."

"Did you go check on Flea and Ty, or to determine if the targets had been prosecuted?" Chet pressed.

"Negative," replied Trask. "Milagros saw us as she ran out. She yelled to us that Flea and Ty were dead, so we opted to go after the guy that was chasing her…you know, to back her up."

"The guy heard us coming behind him," Hatch said. "He then jumped my ass, and nearly beat the shit out of me. If it were not for Milagros shooting him, he might have got the best of me. She saved my ass."

Chet found humor in this narrative. His leathery skin cracked with what appeared to be a smile. However, the humorous moment did not last long.

Looking beyond the landing zone, Chet asked, "Where is she?"

"Milagros is dead," said Trask. "I saw her body as we retreated from the grenade blasts."

The lone female Aardvark team member had been an icon to the organization. The men all viewed her as their sister.

Chet reprimanded Hatch, saying, "You ought to be ashamed of yourself." He then loaded his weapon, and said, "Alright, enough of this horseshit. Let's get in and out of there, and remember to kill everyone."

"Goddamn, I love my job," said Trask, as the three of them prepared for their final assault.

❧❧❧

The men bounded across the uneven, rugged terrain, stopping several yards from the building's main entrance.

Chet took charge of this final assault. He was about to order that they split up; to enter the building from multiple locations. However, explosions sounded, and bullets hit the ground and trees around them.

Some of the shots seemed too high to hit them, as evidenced by tree leaves snapping off their branches, caused by the passing projectiles.

Nevertheless, the explosions and ground shots were too close for comfort.

"Get inside, now!" Chet ordered. "We will push forward in unison. Let's get this thing done!"

Chet, Trask, and Hatch moved quickly through the building's main entrance, disappearing into the awaiting abyss.

ૐૐૐ

Papi moved as fast as he could to the lower level of the building, where a BOPS explosive ordinance disposal (EOD) vehicle waited for him.

After tapping on the vehicle to announce his arrival to Haaris, the sole-surviving BOPS agent, Papi opened the passenger door.

"Is the boy secured?" Papi asked.

"Yes, he is," Haaris replied.

Papi entered the vehicle, and worked his way to the rear. He sat down on the edge of a small table, and ran his hand along Nathaniel's forehead, and hair.

Nathaniel was securely fastened in a cot designed for transportation within tight quarters. His eyes were open, but they contained no real signs of life.

Papi sensed a coldness emanate from within them. His heart sank as he pondered the levels of depravity this innocent child had been exposed to throughout this ordeal.

"How is he doing?" Haaris asked.

"Not good," replied Papi. "His head is sweaty, but his skin is ice cold. He is looking at me with those big, beautiful eyes…but there is nothing in them."

As if on cue, Nathaniel, who had yet to utter a single word since the initial attack upon him and his mother in Des Moines, Iowa, placed his hand on Papi's leg.

The gesture brought tears to Papi's eyes. He patted Nathaniel's hand, and said, "Thank you, young man. I love you very much. I am going to keep you safe."

Papi's focus shifted to the plan at hand. He then said to himself, "I hope my boys are safe."

Speaking to Haaris, Papi said, "Cover your ears. It is going to get awfully loud in here really quick."

Papi looked at the detonator Cal had wired together, and thought of Cal's words when he handed it to him:

"Even if you know that we are in harm's way, and with no way out, flip the switch, Pa. If not, those monsters will slaughter the Peña family."

Cal had constructed the device with relative ease. Assembling detonators was one of the many skills he acquired as a member of the elite Delta Force.

Once completed, Cal established a remote connection to a network of traps he planted throughout the compound.

"I prayed, son, that I would not need to use this when you gave it to me," Papi said softly. "Yet, I knew, somewhere deep within my soul, that I would have no choice but to unleash this destruction. I love you boys."

Papi closed his eyes, and flipped the switch.

༉༉༉

"Come on Bo, we can do this, stay with me," Cal grunted, trying to keep Bo on his feet, as he struggled to get them to safety. "Just another couple of feet to the ditch, come on!"

Days earlier, upon settling into the compound, Cal felt somewhat optimistic that the presence of the BOPS team signified the end of this debacle. However, he could not entirely shake the unnerving feeling that he needed to have a contingency plan. He recalled a movie line from some cheesy nineteen ninety's action flick. In that movie, a character stated, "chance favors the prepared mind."

Cal was not certain if it was just some catchy, made-up script line, or if it had basis in a real quote.

"Louis Pasteur," he recalled Papi saying as they watched the flick together, attributing the movie line to a quote from the French microbiologist.

The quote's origination was of no significance to Cal. What mattered was that the concept applied perfectly to their situation. The movie line kept repeating itself in his head, like an old, broken record.

Cal obsessed over preparing for what may or may not be coming their way, and developed a contingency plan.

Cal presupposed that attackers would correctly assess Jennifer and Nathaniel to be located inside the building. Consequently, he rigged each level of the building with enough C-4 explosives to send it flying into the adjoining county.

This was the primary system.

Next, he chose the distance of forty yards from the building to be the official perimeter. He then proceeded to plant the remaining C-4 within the perimeter.

Anyone situated beyond that perimeter, he calculated, would survive the wrath. Anyone caught within that perimeter had practically zero chance of survival.

Finally, Cal layered the land with grenades, gasoline, motor oil, and Claymore antipersonnel mines, just for good measure.

This was the secondary system.

Cal took great care connecting the primary and secondary systems to detonation cords. Each consisted of a high-explosive core, wrapped in a reinforced, waterproof, olive drab plastic coating that, upon remote activation, would transmit an unstoppable detonating wave.

It was a hellacious network of death, meant to deploy only if attackers overran them, leaving them with no option other than defeat.

Now, Cal heard the ground make a sizzling sound, as the detonation cords, and combustible agents he spread about the property, came to life.

This meant only one thing. Papi had initiated the process.

It would only be a matter of seconds before the primary system engaged, and the secondary system, following close behind, would torch most of the earth in their vicinity.

Cal got Bo to the edge of a deep ditch he had previously seen while surveying the landscape. Although the ditch was within the perimeter, it was not laden with explosives, and could provide them with much needed cover.

Cal struggled at getting Bo over the edge, and into the ditch.

Cal kneeled, and used his shoulders and body weight to push Bo, like a football player practicing with a tackle dummy.

Bo slid safely into the ditch, but it was too late for Cal.

An enormous fireball engulfed the surrounding landscape, coupled with noxious fumes. The corresponding hot windblast sent Cal flying beyond the ditch, onto a separate ridge.

The roaring fire, the intense heat, the smells of gasoline and oil, and the sounds of Claymores detonating brought Cal to a different time and place. It was of when he first met Augustus Peña.

As Cal lost consciousness, he whispered the words he always used to label that moment, November fury.

ॐॐॐ

The inbound helicopter, set to arrive at the compound twenty minutes after the one carrying the Aardvarks, shook violently from the blasts. A warning buzzer sounded, and several of the electronics on the dashboard flashed, until the pilot regained control of the helicopter.

"Oh, my God," the pilot said to his co-pilot. He then spoke into his microphone, and reported, "Tower Command, this is Nightingale Five, we have got a mayday, mayday, over."

"Go ahead Nightingale Five. We have you scheduled for final approach at this time. What is your mayday, over?"

"Tower Command, that is an affirmative, we are on our final approach. However, the mayday is not ours. Repeat, mayday is not ours. The landing zone has just erupted into a ball of fire. I am witnessing a massive incendiary event, and it has disrupted our aircraft. Do you copy?"

"Roger, Nightingale Five," replied Tower Command. "We are also receiving similar reports from commercial air traffic controllers in the area. Nightingale Five, you are to return to base. We are dispatching a response team to the site, do you copy?"

"Copy that, Tower Command. Nightingale Five returning to base - out."

ॐॐॐ

The conflagration that came to life after Papi flipped the switch was beyond anything he could have imagined. The rumbling, crackling, and swooshing sounds made the world around him appear biblical, as if the apocalypse had arrived in full force.

Papi knew that he, Haaris, and Nathaniel were safe inside of the EOD vehicle. However, he also knew that his sons were out there…unprotected.

As the inferno around them subsided, Papi reached for the door handle of the EOD vehicle, and started to exit.

"I would really like to know what it is that you think you are about to accomplish?" asked Haaris.

"My boys are out there. I need to go find them. There is no way that they are okay after all of that."

Haaris replied, "We are on a very tight time schedule, Mr. Baker. Your son, Caleb, demanded that we move as quickly as humanly possible if it came to this. Besides, and it is not my intention to be crude here, but you may not like what you find."

"I am aware of our need for speed, and perhaps I will not like what I find," replied Papi. "But I have to go anyway."

દે•દે•દે

Papi covered his face with a rag as he traversed the scorched earth beneath his boots. Although most of the ground around him was no longer on fire, fumes filled the air, and the atmosphere was red hot.

The sound of an approaching helicopter echoed in the distance.

Obsessed with the need to find his boys, Papi pressed further into the torched landscape.

Soon, he came upon a mound of dirt located along what was once a tree line. Papi struggled to navigate up the mound, as the ashen earth beneath him made for poor footing.

Upon reaching the top of the mound, Papi fell to his knees, and cried out, "My boys…Caleb…Bo…Oh, lord, NO!"

At the bottom of a ditch, which opened in front of him, he saw the bodies of his two sons.

They laid there motionless.

Papi cried at the top of his lungs, but no sound emerged from his mouth. He lunged forward with his arms opened wide, and allowed gravity to slide him down the mud to his dead sons.

Papi gently touched their bodies, and finally emitted the heartbreaking wailing sounds of a father who lost all that was worth living for.

He remained face down in the pit with his boys, prepared to die alongside them. Then, he remembered more of what Cal had said to him, prior to the Aardvark invasion of the compound.

"If things get to the point, Pa, where Auggie's family can no longer be protected here, you need to get them to Marshal Dee. She, and her wife, will be the only ones who can keep them alive. Furthermore, Pa, if it does come to this, you must be extremely careful. A demise that big means the official channel of operations is corrupt. Trust no one affiliated with the operation, other than Augustus, of course, and Haaris."

Papi nodded his head, and said, "You're right, Caleb. That is what I need to do."

He ran his hand over both of his sons one last time, and said, "You boys go home to momma now. Tell her that I will be home soon. I love you all to Heaven and back."

Papi stood up, and exited the pit.

⌘⌘⌘

ELEVEN

Although consumed with deep sorrow, Papi did not allow grief to overcome him. He traversed the charred fields quickly, and arrived at the EOD vehicle.

Papi paused before entering, and said, "How in God's name am I going to get Augustus' son to Marshal Dee?"

He looked skywards, and said, "Caleb, son, you sure have placed an amazing burden upon me. Yet, somehow, I do believe that the good Lord will show me the way. Hallelujah, He will show me the way."

≈≈≈

Haaris was shouting into the receiver of his tiny flip phone when Papi entered the EOD vehicle. "I only have forty-five seconds remaining on this phone. Is it a go, or not?"

Papi looked worriedly at Haaris. He had no idea who Haaris was talking to, or why. However, he did not let worry morph into fear. Cal instructed Papi to trust Haaris, and Papi was going to honor his son's directive.

"Yes, it is a go," replied the voice on the other end of the crackling phoneline.

Haaris flipped the phone shut, and looked at Papi with sympathy. He could tell by Papi's body language that his sons did not survive.

Papi sat down, shut the door, and stared blindly out the front window. "They are dead," he finally said. "My boys are gone now to be with their momma."

Snapping from his spell, Papi pointed to Haaris' flip phone, and asked, "What was that all about?"

"Mr. Baker –"

"Papi, please son, just stick to calling me that…please."

"Alright…Papi. I don't know how much Caleb shared with you about the contingency plan. My preference is to explain it all to you before we leave, but we are almost out of time." Haaris said.

"Caleb implored me to trust you. So, if you have something in mind that will get this boy to safety, then quit your yapping, and get it happening." Papi replied.

Haaris nervously nodded multiple times as he started the EOD vehicle, and shifted it into drive…

≈≈≈≈

Thick, black smoke swirled harmoniously as the chopper containing the response team touched down.

"Get the fire suppression plane over this area pronto," the response commander ordered his first lieutenant. "We also need to get a couple of our hot-suit guys into what remains of that building, STAT. Headquarters needs to know the status of the family. Move it!"

The first lieutenant hustled away, and directed several of his men to gear up in Zetex fireproof suits. As they suited up, he briefed them on the commander's order that they enter the smoldering, demolished building, and locate the Peña family.

The men geared up in record pace, and rushed inside.

Several minutes later, the hot-suit team reported via radio to the commander.

"Alpha, this is Dragon Breath. We are inside this inferno, and cannot locate the Peña family. We searched what we believe to have been the common areas of the structure. We are going in deeper. Alpha, the heat, smoke, and debris make it highly unlikely that anyone beyond this point is still alive."

The commander asked, "Can you and your men safely make it further into the structure?"

"Affirmative, sir. Our suits are good for another several hundred degrees."

"Very well, then. Move on in, and report back. Alpha, out."

≈≈≈≈

Haaris cautiously navigated the vehicle across the charred fields. The ground was littered with debris, making for a rough and unstable ride.

"Will these tires hold up?" Papi asked, concerned that the debris would cause a tire to erupt.

"These puppies can withstand just about anything," Haaris replied.

The EOD vehicle crept along the field, and into a fresh clearing, beyond the debris.

Haaris kept the vehicle's speed to no more than ten miles per hour. He remained vigilant, constantly scanning their surroundings.

"I thought you said we were on a time crunch," grumbled Papi.

"We are," Haaris replied. "I will explain it to you when we…"

An armed man seemingly appeared out of nowhere in the path ahead of them.

Haaris slammed the brakes.

Papi swallowed hard.

Haaris stared intensely at the man, trying to determine if he were friend, or foe.

The man looked all around him, then made a hand gesture towards the EOD vehicle.

Haaris did not hesitate, and responded by making a different hand gesture.

The man waved the EOD vehicle through his position, allowing them to pass, as if they were at a checkpoint.

Haaris and the man locked eyes, and nodded at each other, as the EOD vehicle pressed forward into the hostile world beyond.

ঌঌঌ

The road which the mysterious, armed man waved them onto was mostly dirt, and rock.

Haaris maintained his speed. He did this to avoid attracting attention by kicking up dirt along his path.

Visibly agitated, Papi asked, "Are we getting to that point, young man, where you explain to me what the dickens is going on here? Who was that man? What is with those hand signals you both gave to each other? Where are we going, and why are we driving so dagnabbit slow over this field?"

"Okay," replied Haaris. "Alright. Of course, you need to know. I get it. But you should know that I am focusing on getting us far enough away before I take off like a bat out of Hell."

Papi gave him a look of bewilderment. Although Cal had specifically named Haaris as someone to be trusted, Papi also recalled Cal's warning. No one could be trusted. Papi wanted to trust Haaris, but he had seen too much, and suffered too greatly to drop his guard. *This is a great quandary,"* Papi thought.

Haaris noticed the concern on Papi's face, and said, "Caleb and I both agreed, as he put this plan together, that if it came to the predicament we currently find ourselves in, that the official channels of operation have become irreparably corrupted. I believed it then, and I believe it now. Because of this, Papi, I am doing all that I can to avoid detection from those in our government that have already killed Mrs. Peña, and for some ungodly reason, want to kill her toddler son."

Papi continued pressing Haaris. "How can you claim you are avoiding detection when we have already been identified? That armed man back there had the same uniform on as you. He works for the government, too, does he not? And what was with those mumbo jumbo hand gestures you both did before he sent us this way?"

"Caleb and I are not only U.S. Army Delta brothers-in-arms," Haaris answered, "but we are also bonded through an ancient fraternal order. It is through this unofficial channel, an underground network of bonded souls if you would, that will save this boy's life. This is as much as I can share with you, Mr. Baker...ugh, I mean, Papi. Please, trust me. I have faith that we will prevail, and that this boy will survive."

"An ancient fraternal order you say, huh?" Papi mused. "Well, by God this day isn't ever going to get less bizarre, is it?"

⌘⌘⌘

TWELVE

Haaris picked up his phone as it buzzed. He then drove to a relatively large boulder, and parked the EOD vehicle alongside it for concealment.

"It's him," Haaris told Papi.

"Who, the hand-signaling fellow we passed back there?" Papi asked.

"Yes," Haaris replied. He then flipped open his phone, and took the call.

Haaris mainly listened, occasionally offering a quick acknowledgment by uttering "uh, huh."

Finally, Haaris said, "I know exactly where that is. I attended Mass there several days ago upon my arrival to this area. We will go there tonight, under the cover of darkness. Thank you, brother."

Haaris looked back at Nathaniel, who was squirming slightly. He then looked at Papi, and said, "I think the little guy needs to go to the bathroom. I have several 24-hour diapers stashed throughout this truck. I will take care of it."

"You're a very kindhearted individual," Papi said with slight sarcasm. "But what I am really interested in is the context of the telephone conversation you just had. What gives?"

"The woman who will raise this boy as her own will meet us this evening. She will place him under her protection, and take him to safety."

"Marshal Dee is coming here tonight?" Papi asked.

"That is correct," replied Haaris. "However, as I am sure you are aware, she is no longer a Deputy U.S. Marshal."

"Yes, I know, I know," replied Papi. "It's just old habits, is all. Those motherless bastards in Washington did wrong by Dee. They passed her up for promotions, and kept her away from high-profile assignments seeing as how she is a gay woman. Caleb told me all about it. He was red-hot mad about it too, let me tell you. He had a great deal of respect, and admiration, for that woman. Caleb was heartbroken when Dee was forced to resign."

"Which is undoubtedly why Cal entrusted her to undertake the responsibility of raising Nathaniel," Haaris offered.

"I'm curious," said Papi. "Did the plan for Nathaniel being raised by Dee involve his mother at all? She was alive when Caleb put this plan together."

"The plan for Jennifer," Haaris answered, "was a little more complex. She was to be sent to a Convent in Mexico while she healed. Afterwards, she was to be moved to a church parish not far from where Nathaniel is to be raised. She would then have visits with Nathaniel on holy ground, under the auspices of furthering his religious education."

"I did not know the woman very well," said Papi. "Nevertheless, I am deeply saddened by her death. I know how much Augustus loved her. I am convinced, though, that she would greatly approve of your plan for little Nate's raising."

Haaris began making his way to Nathaniel, to change his diaper, when Papi asked where they would be meeting up with Dee.

"She will meet us at the Saint Michael Mission, which is located not far from here, in the town of Naco, Arizona."

෨෨෨෨

Stitch sat on the ground with his back against a tree stump. His legs were bent, allowing him to rest his head on his knees. Cradling his bent legs with his left arm, Stitch stretched out his right arm to allow a responding medic to check his vitals.

"I'm fine," Stitch said, shifting his position slightly.

"Stay still," said the medic. "You know better than to talk and move while I check your blood pressure."

"Go ahead, do your thing," Stitch replied, agitated by all that had happened.

Stitch had been exposed to bloodshed throughout his career, and was typically not disturbed by it. But this was different. The energy surrounding this area reeked of pure evil. He felt nervous, as if he had done something bad. He could not place a finger on it. The deaths of all these people, which likely included a mother, and her child, sickened him. He did not vomit, though. Instead, after the medic completed his checks, Stitch hugged his legs tight with both arms, and cried uncontrollably into his knees.

࿏࿏࿏

The men wearing the Zetex fireproof suits emerged from what remained of the smoldering building.

"Sir, we have several KIA in there," one of the men reported to the first lieutenant. "We were able to make out five enemy combatants, based on what remained of their protective armor. Unfortunately, we were also able to confirm the death of a female non-combatant, which I assess to be the mother."

"The child?" The first lieutenant hesitantly asked.

"We were unable to locate the child. The heat was taking our suits beyond their capacity, preventing us from pressing further than the mother. Lieutenant, nothing beyond that point is alive. There is absolutely no chance of survival. I'm sorry."

"I agree with his assessment," said another man who took part of the search inside the structure. "However, the bodies are in pretty bad shape from being scorched. Positive identification will take some time."

The first lieutenant acknowledged their assessments with a nod, and said, "I am also receiving reports of KIA's outside the structure. Not all of them are enemy combatants, as I understand it."

After a brief pause, the first lieutenant said, "Good work, gentlemen. Get yourselves out of those suits. There is nothing left in there for you to find."

The first lieutenant approached the response team commander, and briefed him on what he learned.

"Understood," the commander solemnly replied.

The commander slowly spun in a full 360 degrees circle, observing his response team recover the remains of the fallen BOPS agents.

He then told the first lieutenant, "Notify BOPS headquarters we have confirmed there are zero survivors, to include the family."

The first lieutenant acknowledged the order, and left.

"A terrible battle was fought here today," the commander softly said. "Everyone here died performing their duty. It was good versus evil.

The commander removed his helmet, and took a knee on the crunchy earth beneath him.

"I cannot fathom why all of this has occurred," he said in prayer. "I feel as if my soul has been degraded by simply witnessing all of this."

The commander looked skywards, and said, "Lord, I am not worthy that you should enter under my roof. But only say the word, and my soul shall be healed."

⌘⌘⌘

THIRTEEN

At 9:30 p.m., Haaris resumed driving the EOD vehicle.

"Saint Michael's Mission is about forty minutes away," Haaris said to Papi.

"Okay," replied Papi. "So, are you planning on driving up to it, and parking this thing right out front? It is not exactly an inconspicuous vehicle, you know?"

"Of course not," Haaris chuckled. "But not for the reasons you may think."

"How's that?" Papi queried.

"The Mission is situated 1.8 miles from the U.S. Customs and Border Protection's border crossing station. Consequently, this type of vehicle is not so uncommon in these parts." Haaris explained.

"I'm not reading you," said Papi.

"The town of Naco," Haaris continued, "is an official border crossing town. Because of this fact, the locals are accustomed to seeing federal law enforcement vehicles of all types, including those used in support of anti-terrorist operations, such as the bomb disposal truck we are currently in."

"So, you are suggesting that we are good in here then?" Papi asked.

"That is correct," replied Haaris. "We most certainly are. However, as part of our plan to get little Nathaniel to safety, we are going to make a vehicle switch prior to arriving at the Mission."

"I am intrigued," Papi mused.

"There will be a van waiting for us at an abandoned U.S. Army Fort called Camp Naco. The van will be fueled up, and ready to go with fresh supplies. It is approximately three minutes from the Mission."

"By fresh supplies, do you mean food and water?" Papi asked.

"Yes," Haaris answered. "In addition to supplies for Nathaniel, and new weapons with ammunition for us."

"I like this plan," Papi said. "Let's get moving."

や や や

Camp Naco was the only remaining military compound of approximately a dozen that were established along the U.S./Mexican border during the Mexican Revolution of 1910 to 1920. Although officially closed in 1923, and subsequently used as a Civilian Conservation Corps camp in the 1930's, the compound had been largely abandoned ever since.

The EOD vehicle crept to what was once the Fort's main entrance. A perimeter fence now surrounded the compound, designed to keep visitors from entering the grounds, as access to the buildings that remain standing was off limits to the public.

"This place is a ghost town," Papi whispered.

"There is a lot of history here," replied Haaris. "As I understand it, this is where the U.S. Army stationed the 9th and 10th Cavalry Regiments, as well as the 25th Infantry Regiment. These were all Buffalo Soldier units."

"Isn't that something," Papi said, admiring the vast, abandoned military compound that once housed the Black Cavalry soldiers nicknamed Buffalo Soldiers by Native American tribes during the Indian Wars.

A light flickered ahead in the distance.

"Is that meant for us?" Papi asked.

"That's our cue," acknowledged Haaris, who then flickered his headlights three times.

Two men dashed from a quad of buildings that appeared to be former barracks. The men opened the fence, and waved the EOD vehicle through.

As he cautiously drove to where he saw the flickering light, Haaris looked in his rearview mirror. He observed the men close the gate, and retreat into the building from which they emerged.

Haaris stopped the EOD vehicle alongside a building that had once been the officers' quarters. He then lowered his window to speak with the individual who had shone the light at him.

"There is a horse stable around the corner of this building," the person said. "The van is ready to go, brother. We will help you unload so that you may quickly continue on this quest."

Before Haaris could reply, the individual vanished into the darkness.

❧❧❧

"Those boys were awful quick at getting us squared away in this van," Papi said.

"They are unquestionably as committed as I am at completing this mission," replied Haaris.

"Speaking of missions," Papi said, "we should be there any moment."

Haaris nodded, and said, "Here we are."

Haaris made a right turn into the mission's driveway, and parked at the rear.

A nun appeared at the back door with a large cart.

"Thank you for delivering these much-needed supplies," she smilingly said to Haaris and Papi. She then entered the van, and began placing items on the cart.

As the nun prepared to return into the mission with the cart full of supplies, she said, "Be ready to load the child onto this cart when I return. I covered him with blankets to conceal him."

Haaris and Papi complied, and loaded Nathaniel onto the supply cart upon the nun's return, in addition to several other items from the van.

❧❧❧

The interior of the Saint Michael Mission was simple. White walls, dark brown ceiling fans, a handful of crucifixes and statues, and colonial maple wood pews greeted those who came here seeking the Grace of God.

Haaris, Papi, and the nun moved quickly to get the cart that Nathaniel laid upon to the altar.

The supply cart's wheels squeaked with each revolution, causing an echo within the church.

Seated in the front pew, facing the altar, was a tall woman, cloaked in a white hooded robe. Upon hearing the cart, and the hurried footsteps that accompanied it, the woman blessed herself by making the sign of the cross, and turned to greet everyone.

Rising to her feet, she said, "Mr. Baker, it is an honor to meet you. Your son Cal always spoke so highly of you." She paused for a second before saying, "I heard about your sons. I have no words to offer other than to thank you for raising such wonderful human beings."

"Marshal Dee," Papi said, holding back tears. He wanted to say more, but he simply could not.

Dee continued. "This saint of a woman is Sister Kathleen. None of this would have been possible without her amazing faith, and her incredible gift at employing it."

Sister Kathleen bowed her head, saying, "Thank you."

Dee walked to the cart, and removed the blanket that covered Nathaniel. Looking at the boy, she said, "I met his father, but never his mother. I cannot believe..."

Dee caught herself before bursting into tears as she was about to address the murder of the boy's mother. She turned her head away, and caught her composure.

Holding onto Nathaniel's hand, Dee said, "I cannot claim with an honest heart that I believe God is proud of the choices I have made in my life. But I promise, Nathaniel, that you, God, and your beautiful mother will revere the life I have planned for you, and the man that you will become. I will love you, protect you, and guide you to be the best example of what God expects of his children."

Dee then bent over, and kissed Nathaniel on his forehead.

Papi welled up with emotion. The interaction between Dee and Nathaniel reminded him of his boys. He could not shake the images appearing in his mind of Caleb and Bo as newborns, as toddlers, as young boys, and as the men *they* had become.

The feeling was overwhelming, and made Papi dizzy, causing him to sit clumsily into the nearest pew.

"Papi, are you okay?" Haaris asked, alarmed.

"I am doing just fine. Don't you go making a fuss about nothing. It has been a long day is all. I need to just sit here, and rest." Papi protested.

"I will bring you some blankets, food, and water," said Sister Kathleen. "You can stretch out on this pew, and get some sleep. It is nice and wide, you need not worry about falling off," she said jokingly. "We are staying here overnight, and are leaving at seven in the morning. I will come wake you up, so don't you worry about setting any kind of alarms."

"Thank you, sister," Papi replied.

As she left, Papi grabbed her arm and said, "Sister, I would be more than grateful if you would say some prayers with me after bringing the blankets, and food."

Sister Kathleen replied, "But of course, Mr. Baker. Do you have anything particular in mind?"

"I was hoping to recite Psalm 27:3, and Joshua 1:9 if you don't mind too much," said Papi.

"And so it shall be," replied Sister Kathleen, as she departed to get Papi his blankets, and food.

అంఅంఅం

At precisely 5:30 a.m., Sister Kathleen made her way through the Saint Michael Mission to gently wake everyone for the day's journey.

Having roused everyone, including Nathaniel, she went to the pew where Papi had fallen asleep.

Sister Kathleen gently nudged Papi, encouraging him to wake up. After a few unsuccessful attempts, she became worried, and placed her hand on Papi's forehead, and neck.

Sister Kathleen dropped to her knees, and started to pray.

Seeing this, Haaris and Dee came to her.

"Is something wrong?" Haaris asked.

"No," Sister Kathleen replied. "In fact, it is quite the opposite. This man has moved on to be with his family, and with God."

"We saw you praying with him last night," Haaris said. "I took him at his word when he said he was exhausted when he abruptly dropped onto the pew. Did he say anything to you about how he felt?"

"The only thing he said to me, other than the prayers, was a phrase in Latin," replied Sister Kathleen.

"What was the phrase?" Dee asked.

Sister Kathleen answered, "He said, Quam ut moriatur quod secretum. It translates into the secret is how to die."

అంఅంఅం

Dee, Haaris, and Nathaniel were set to leave.

Sister Kathleen hugged Dee, bidding farewell.

"I will report this man's death to the authorities in another two hours," said Sister Kathleen.

"His identity will be revealed," said Haaris. "Everyone believes he died during the mercenary raid, along with his sons, and the Peña family. His death in this location will generate chaos for them, and great problems for you, sister."

"I answer only to God," Sister Kathleen replied. "There is no sin in protecting the life of this child from the monsters who are hunting him."

"It is time to go," Dee said.

恓恓恓

Nathaniel sat at the rear of the van. He seemed almost cheerful as he ate animal crackers while sipping on some juice, and looking out the window.

Haaris checked his 9mm handgun, chambered a round, and placed the weapon into safety mode. He looked over at Dee, and asked, "Are you ready?"

Dee replied, "Yes. I was born to do this."

⌘⌘⌘

FOURTEEN

NORTH DAKOTA

The man in charge of the XM team currently located on Trent Chism's property was named Jericho.

Growing impatient, he paced about, looking at his watch.

"This is taking way too long," he said to the men assembled around him. "I'll give him three more minutes to report his status before I absolutely lose my mind, and go take care of this myself."

He then stormed towards one of the SUVs parked in the field.

"Boss," shouted a woman from the parked helicopter. "We have Belize on the wire. They need to speak with you."

"Good," he replied. "At least someone feels it is important to communicate with me."

"This is Jericho," he said angrily into the radio's handset.

"Mission aborted. The client has become hostile, and reports they have eradicated our inbound assets. You are to exfiltrate from client's jurisdiction at once, and return to Belize," said the voice on the other side of the line.

Jericho tossed the handset aside and whistled loudly.

The team pulled in close to him as he spoke.

"We are on a hot retreat. Belize says that we have gone from predators to prey. This goose is cooked. We are popping smoke, and getting out of here."

Curious about the assassin sent to kill Trent Chism, one of the men queried, "What about Aziz?"

"I can only assume, based on what Belize told me, that Aziz is dead," replied Jericho.

The team collectively acknowledged, and returned to their vehicles for a rapid departure.

ॐॐॐ

Trent Chism sat in the rear seat of his pickup truck as Augustus drove. Across his lap, lied a bolt-action sniper rifle. His body swayed sideways as Augustus drove over the rugged ranchland.

Looking at the rifle, Trent said, "You realize, don't you, that I only collect these guns. I don't actually know how to shoot most of them, especially this one."

"That's perfect," replied Augustus. "I prefer to do all of the killing on my missions."

Trent gazed solemnly out the window.

"Don't worry, buddy," Augustus said. "I am not going to hurt you. Although it is true, that knowing me will probably get you killed, I will not be the one to end your life."

Trent shifted his gaze back to Augustus. He then chuckled softly, while shaking his head, and said, "You really do have a way of cheering people up."

"I'm glad you feel that way," said Augustus, "because I'm about to bring you down again."

Trent shrugged his shoulders, inquisitively looked at Augustus, and asked, "What now?"

"I am picking up some chatter on the radio I took from the man I killed at your home. They are leaving. I cannot tell if their intent is to abandon that man, or if they have learned of his demise. It is very unlikely that they would abandon him, which leads me to believe they might be onto us," said Augustus.

Trent looked at the weapon across his lap again, and muttered, "I suppose it's finally time for me to learn how to shoot my guns."

෯෯෯

Although driving with his headlights off, Augustus remained concerned with the limited concealment of his approach.

The open plains were not conducive to sneak raids, especially against a vigilant adversary. Augustus suspected the mercenaries would routinely scan their surroundings with binoculars, to identify any approaching threats.

Augustus stopped driving, and grabbed a pair of binoculars he acquired from Trent's arsenal. He peered at the enemy in the distance, and observed the group preparing to retreat.

Their fleeing emboldened him.

"Regardless of whether or not they learned of their comrades' demise, one thing is for certain. They are spooked, and not on their full guard." Augustus said.

Augustus exited the truck.

He opened the rear door, and said to Trent, "Give me the rifle. Also, pass me that canvas bag, slowly."

Trent handed him the rifle. He then grabbed the canvas bag.

Holding the canvas bag outward with a stretched arm, he looked frighteningly at Augustus and asked, "Are these what I think they are?"

"Grenades, yes; that is exactly what they are. Do you have a problem with that? I mean, they are yours." Augustus replied.

"Just take them, and get this over with," said Trent, hurriedly.

Augustus took the canvas bag and, along with the sniper rifle, scurried to position himself closer to the retreating group ahead of him.

ॐॐॐ

Jericho rapped several times on the side of the helicopter. Appearing in front of the craft's windshield, he gave a thumbs-up signal to the pilots.

Without delay, the helicopter hummed as it came to life.

Next, Jericho displayed four fingers to the pilots, while mouthing to them that he would return in four minutes.

Jericho turned, and jogged to the SUV parked closest to him. He wanted to speak with the driver. However, he stopped upon observing a distinctive crack in the SUVs windshield. It was more of a hole, about the circumference of a silver dollar.

"Oh, no," said Jericho.

He inched closer, and confirmed his fear.

The driver was dead, killed by a single shot that removed the top of his skull.

Jericho frantically motioned for the two remaining SUVs to get moving. He sighed from relief when they complied, happy to know they were still alive. However, his relief ended quickly.

The windshield on the SUV furthest from him puffed twice, with what looked like dust.

Jericho knew what he saw was not dust. Rather, it represented two bullets popping through the glass.

The SUV maneuvered erratically and, eventually, came to a halt. The rear occupants exited the vehicle with their weapons drawn.

Jericho then witnessed the remaining SUV come under assault.

The sounds of tires exploding, and glass shattering, filled the air. Within moments, those XM operators still alive were out in the open, shooting in every direction.

The ruckus of automatic weapons fire lessened by the second, as his men were methodically executed by this ghost of a killer.

In a desperate act of self-preservation, Jericho turned and ran for the helicopter. As he ran, a shot hit the ground in front of him. He immediately stopped, dropped, and rolled.

"Where is the goddamned shooter?" He yelled aloud to himself.

Suddenly, he heard the helicopter begin its ascent. "No, wait!" he shouted.

Jericho did not have his weapon on him. He had secured it inside the chopper, in anticipation of lifting off with them soon. If they left, he would be defenseless.

Jericho stood up, and took a couple of steps forward.

PFFFT...sounded the dirt in front of him, as a bullet entered the earth.

"Fuck!" Jericho screamed, diving again onto the ground. He remained motionless, and saw activity to his right. He focused hard on where he saw the movement, and observed his menace.

"What in the name of...?" Jericho exclaimed, seeing the figure jump onto the helicopter skids.

Feeling somewhat certain that this man represented the only shooter, Jericho stood up, and ran to the rising helicopter.

But Jericho stopped just as quickly as he started when he saw what the man was doing.

"Sonofabitch," Jericho shouted, as he dropped to the ground yet again. This time, he covered his ears.

Jericho glanced upwards through squinted eyes, anticipating a blast.

Instead, he saw the man drop to the ground, and roll away into the darkness.

࿊ ࿊ ࿊

Augustus masterfully hunted his prey. He needed to move swiftly, or they would all be gone in a matter of moments. Adrenaline rushed through his veins. He welcomed every bit of it, like a junkie on heroin.

Augustus thrived in moments like this. He had a reputation for completing tasks with an unmatched professional zeal.

Slowing his pace, Augustus identified his first target.

From what Augustus could see through the rifle's scope, the driver of the SUV on his left was the lone occupant of that vehicle.

The two SUV's to his right had at least three passengers each, in addition to its driver.

Augustus also took mental notes of a man addressing the helicopter crew. "That must be their leader. I will need to capture him. But first, I need to take care of these guys." Augustus decided to attack the lone occupant first.

Augustus picked up his pace for the final assault. He then slid to the ground, like a baseball player stealing second base, while holding his rifle in a shooting position.

Upon completing his slide, he inhaled an even, short breath. Augustus clenched his teeth, and unleashed his lethal shot.

The rifle was equipped with a modified suppressor, causing the typical roar of the weapon to fall silent.

Augustus kept his sights on the driver, to confirm his kill. Upon seeing the top of the driver's head disappear, Augustus switched his focus to his remaining targets. He made quick work of them.

He then looked to the man he presumed to be the group's leader.

The man was hauling ass to the helicopter.

Augustus mockingly said, "No, no, no. What do you think you are doing?"

To keep the man at bay, Augustus fired at his feet.

As Augustus had presumed, the man responded by employing evasive maneuvers, disrupting his path to the helicopter.

When the man dropped to the ground to avoid the shots, Augustus darted to the helicopter.

Swinging the rifle's harness over his shoulder, Augustus leapt, grabbing ahold of the helicopter skids.

The aircraft was taking off.

Augustus secured his legs around the skid, and reached into his jacket pocket. He then pulled out two grenades, removed their pins, and tapped on the half-opened compartment door.

The pilots turned to look, and Augustus said, "It is extremely disloyal to leave your man behind. Here is your punishment."

Augustus then tossed the grenades inside, in separate directions, and dropped to the ground below.

As the sounds of the exploding helicopter echoed into the North Dakota night sky, Augustus said, "I got one back in your honor, buddy," referring to the pilot recently killed by the missiles.

Without skipping a beat, Augustus stood up, and marched to retrieve his prisoner.

෴෴෴

Augustus unholstered his .45 caliber pistol. As he closed in on his soon to be prisoner, he shot the ground around the motionless man.

"Don't play possum with me," shouted Augustus. "I am known for shooting the dead, just to make sure they stay that way. The next shot is to your head, in case you were wondering about my intentions."

Without waiting for a response, Augustus cocked the gun's hammer, and took the shot.

The bullet came so close to his head, that Jericho swore the round struck him. Jericho instantly spun onto his back, begging for his life.

"Stop," he cried. "Okay, I get it. I'm dead, right? Please, don't freaking kill me man. I have a young boy at home. Please."

The mere mention of his son, as a reason to spare his life, set Augustus off. He dropped down onto both his knees. Using the downward momentum, he crashed the butt of his gun against Jericho's forehead.

He then grabbed Jericho by the throat. With a vicelike grip, he pulled Jericho to him, and snarled, "I am here, because the people you work for tried to kill me, my wife, and my toddler son. Do not think for a moment that I give a rat's ass about your son growing up without his father. If you do not give me what I need, your son will experience the same grief that my son currently suffers from every day - the anguish of losing his father. Do I make myself clear you pathetic, sonofabitch?"

Jericho's affirmation was barely audible, due to Augustus' choking grip.

"Good," said Augustus. "If you want to live, start taking off your clothing. If you want to die, ask me why. It is entirely up to you."

Augustus cocked the gun's hammer once more, making sure Jericho saw him do it. He then released his grip from Jericho's throat.

There was no question in Jericho's mind that Augustus was serious. Jericho wholeheartedly wanted to get home to his son. He was not going to tempt fate, so he stripped.

Augustus watched Jericho remove his clothing in the blistering cold night. *What a pussy,* thought Augustus. *I would have fought to the death instead of stripping.*

He then unclipped a two-way radio from his belt.

"We are good to go, pal," said Augustus. "Come get us."

Seconds later, Trent's pickup truck barreled towards them at full speed.

⌘⌘⌘

FIFTEEN

Augustus held up both his arms, waving Trent to him.

Trent stopped the truck, got out, and hustled to Augustus. "Is it all over? Did you get what you needed? Should I call the authorities?"

"Bro," said Augustus, "you need to chill out."

"Why is that man taking off his clothing?" Trent shouted.

"Because he is some sort of freak, I don't know. Why don't you ask him?" Quipped Augustus.

Trent stared incredulously at the now naked Jericho.

Augustus continued to speak. "Didn't you say you have a friend who lives somewhere around here, that has Special Forces experience?"

"He is more of an acquaintance," Trent replied. "I wouldn't go so far as to call him my friend."

"Friend; acquaintance; who gives a shit?" Augustus shot back. "He will be very useful. Take me to him."

"I don't know," Trent protested. "He is not one that takes kindly to outsiders. I don't think that is such a good idea."

"Good idea or not," said Augustus, "it is the only one I have. So, unless you want to be responsible for this prisoner, I suggest you get us to your bestie as soon as possible."

"He is not my bestie," Trent scoffed. "And why in the world is that man butt naked!?"

Augustus looked at Jericho, then back to Trent, and said, "Because I told him to strip."

He then grabbed Jericho by the back of his neck, and escorted him to Trent's truck.

❧❧❧

Jonah Spraggs lied in bed, gazing up at the ceiling. He could not fall asleep.

Sleep typically did not come easily to Jonah. Yet, he found his inability to snooze this evening particularly troubling.

"I doubt looking at adult magazines will help, but who knows?" he said.

Jonah turned to his nightstand. He rummaged through it, and retrieved a copy of Big Booty magazine. He unenthusiastically flipped through a few pages, using the moonlight that shined through his window for illumination.

"Nope," he said, tossing the magazine to the floor. "There is nothing here for me tonight."

Feeling the warmth of sleep finally come over him, Jonah closed his eyes in eager anticipation. However, his journey into the joyous realm of sleep ended abruptly; interrupted, by a long, sustained honk of a car horn.

Jonah sat up in bed so fast, he felt lightheaded. As he waited for his lightheadedness to subside, the horn outside sounded yet again.

"What stupid, shit for brains asshole, is out there honking like that?" He shouted, cupping both his ears with his palms.

When the honking stopped, Jonah stood up, and bolted out his room to greet this nuisance in person.

As he reached his front door, Jonah retrieved a heavy bust of Nero from a coffee table. Enraged at the audacity of the bastard who kept honking the horn, Jonah opened the front door, and hurled the bust at the vehicle.

The bust smashed into Trent's windshield.

"Oh, shit," exclaimed Trent, instinctively covering his face with his arms.

"This guy is seriously pissed off," said Augustus, looking at the car horn he just finished depressing. "I guess we should have called?"

Trent opened the passenger door, saying, "We are just lucky he didn't come out with a flamethrower or something. Let me handle this. I will get him calmed down."

"Hey, Jonah, it's me, Trent Chism. You know…the guy who won't let his cows be eaten?"

Jonah's rage was still present. However, he addressed Trent with great respect, and with what appeared to be admiration.

"Mr. Chism," said Jonah. "Why in God's name would you do this to me? I would not go to your home, in the middle of the night, and disturb you like you just did to me."

"You would if you needed my help to stay alive," replied Trent.

Jonah's posture stiffened. His breathing was rapid, but no longer from rage. Instead, he found himself consumed with great concern for Trent and his safety.

"What do you mean, Mr. Chism? Is your life in danger? What is going on? Are you hurt?"

"I am fine for now," said Trent. "But I may not be for much longer." Trent motioned to his truck. "I need you to meet someone. I only recently met him. Tonight actually, but he has already saved my life."

Jonah appeared agitated, and extremely uncomfortable with the thought of meeting someone new.

"I know how difficult it is for you to meet strangers, and trust them, Jonah. I really do. But, please, I need your help, man," Trent pleaded.

Jonah nodded in agreement, while also spreading his arms out, suggesting he did not know what else to do but to acquiesce to Trent's plea for help.

"There is one more thing," said Trent. "He has a prisoner with him."

≈≈≈

Jonah approached the truck, running his hands over his head. He stopped upon making eye contact with Augustus.

Understanding this was a sensitive moment for Jonah, Augustus moved cautiously. He showed Jonah both hands through the windshield, to reveal he was not holding a weapon. He then pointed to the driver's door, to signal he intended to exit the truck.

Jonah acknowledged both gestures with a slow nod, and Augustus got out.

"My name is Augustus Peña. According to what Trent has told me, you and I share a common interest. More importantly, we share an uncommon bond."

"Yeah, what are those?" Jonah queried.

"Well, although I do not know the exact details of your experiences, it does seem that you have been exposed to, shall we say, things the average citizen knows nothing about."

"Go on," Jonah said, cautiously.

"You are a former special operator for the US military, are you not?" Augustus asked.

"I am," replied Jonah.

"Well, me too, sort of," said Augustus. "I have spent much of my adult life working in the shadows, on behalf of our country. Forgive me for being slight on the specifics. But what I can tell you, is that my duties have placed me alongside of special operators from each branch of the military. My specialty is targeted assassination. Wet work if you are familiar with that term."

"Doesn't that term refer more to torture, and interrogation, than it does to assassination?" Jonah skeptically asked.

"Good, you know your shit. Now, let's get down to business. Time is of the essence." Augustus replied.

The non-answer irked Jonah, and it showed on his face.

Augustus addressed Jonah's frustration. "Look, I need your help, and the clock is ticking fast. I promise to give you bits and pieces along the way. But right now, I have someone in custody who is instrumental to my finding out what the exact plan is for targeting my family and I for assassination."

Jonah looked at the truck, and said, "In there?"

"Yes, in there," Augustus answered loudly.

Jonah said, "Alright, if Mr. Chism believes in you, then I'm not going to fuss with you too much. But I will need some answers, and quick."

"You got it," said Augustus. He then led Jonah to the rear of the truck.

Augustus pulled back a black tarp that covered the cabin, to reveal his prize.

"Why is he naked?" Jonah asked.

"Because it is freaking freezing out here, and I figured he wouldn't try too hard to escape with nothing on," replied Augustus.

"Intense, but yeah, I get it," said Jonah. "Let's bring him into my shed."

"Is there anyone else here with you?" Augustus asked.

"Nope, just me," replied Jonah.

"Perfect," said Augustus. "Let's go."

❧❧❧

The three men escorted Jericho to the shed. He was barely able to walk, and trembled uncontrollably.

"Are you shaking because you are cold, or because you are about to crap all over yourself?" Augustus asked Jericho.

"Both," muttered Jericho.

"Good," replied Augustus, "then I have your attention." He knelt down by Jericho, and said, "No matter how you slice it, you and your crew were here to support not only the effort of my assassination, but the slaughter of my wife, and son. Now, what I need from you is information. You need to tell me what you were waiting for, and where you were going once you obtained it."

Jericho stared blindly towards the ground without saying a word.

"I was in a chopper earlier tonight," said Augustus. "It got shot out of the sky by a couple of missiles. I was supposed to be onboard when it exploded. Luckily for me, I had the pilot put me down prior to his scheduled landing."

Augustus grabbed Jericho by the throat, choked him hard, and growled, "I presume, that the pilot was bringing me to you."

Augustus let go of his throat.

Jericho coughed violently, but did not answer.

Augustus stood up, and addressed Jonah, "This motherfucker represents a part of Uncle Sam that you do not want to believe exists, but does. All that you have done to serve your country, Jonah, means nothing to a maggot like him. He will dispose of you, slaughter your family, and assassinate your character once you are dead, just to cover his tracks. If you do not help me extract the information I need from him, then everything you have suffered for, in the name of duty, honor, and country, will be wiped away by the atrocities he and his comrades are perpetrating against my family, and I."

Jonah shook with anger, and dove onto Jericho without warning.

"Oh, shit! I did not see that coming," exclaimed Augustus, shocked by the sudden outburst of aggression.

Jonah swiftly placed Jericho in a headlock, squeezing with the strength of a python.

Augustus noticed that Jericho had lost consciousness. Fearful that Jonah would kill him, Augustus shouted at the top of his lungs, "STOP!"

The roar from Augustus startled Jonah, and he complied with the command.

Jonah let go, and Jericho fell over like a bag of sand.

"I can appreciate your enthusiasm, but I need him alive," said Augustus.

Jonah spit on Jericho as he rose to his feet. "Piece of shit," he said.

"When he wakes up," said Augustus, "I am going to take the lead on this. I need you to help me with whatever I ask of you, but do not take matters into your own hands. Got it?"

"Yeah, I got it," grumbled Jonah.

Augustus said, "Good, let's wake this asshole up then, shall we?"

❧❧❧

Augustus straddled Jericho as he lied unconscious on his back. He then sat on Jericho's sternum, and pulled a handkerchief from his jacket, rolling it into a ball. Next, Augustus opened Jericho's mouth and placed the balled-up handkerchief into it. Augustus then placed one hand over Jericho's mouth, while sticking two fingers from his other hand into Jericho's nostrils.

"What in the world?" Trent exclaimed.

"That is some real deal shit," said Jonah, admiring Augustus' work.

"This simulates a sort of panic attack. Like what people with sleep apnea experience when they stop breathing during sleep. Typically, when they stop breathing, they wake up, and jump out of bed, gasping for air," Augustus explained.

"What happens to those who aren't typical?" Trent asked.

"They die," said Augustus.

Looking at Jonah, Augustus said, "If that happens, we can thank the mixed martial arts grand master over here."

Augustus felt some movement come from Jericho.

"Never mind, he is about to join us," Augustus said with a smirk.

With a violent thrash, Jericho's body spasmed, and twisted, until his subconscious mind could no longer contain itself. Like a drowned swimmer returning to life by resuscitation, Jericho gasped, vomited and spit in every direction.

"Relax," Augustus said to him. "It only gets worse from here."

Jericho raised both his hands into the air, as if he were surrendering, saying, "No, no, no."

"Then grow a set of balls, mister field operative, and tell me what it was you were waiting for, and where you were going once you obtained it?" Augustus demanded.

"A lottery ticket," Jericho answered. "It is worth a lot of money."

Augustus raised one eyebrow and glared at Jericho, suggesting that he needed to know more.

Jericho responded to the look, saying, "It is worth significantly more money than what the client was paying for completion of the contract."

Augustus pulled his knife out of its sheath. He grabbed Jericho's head, and sliced off his right ear.

Jericho's screams echoed into the stormy night.

"The contract you refer to in such a cavalier manner was for murdering my wife, my two-year-old son, and me."

Augustus tossed the severed ear aside like a piece of garbage, and said to Jonah, "Given your background, I assume you have first aid supplies."

"I do," replied Jonah, excitedly.

"Good," Augustus said. "Patch him up before he dies of shock due to loss of blood."

Jonah bolted inside his house to obtain the supplies necessary to stabilize Jericho.

Augustus sat cross-legged on the ground.

Trent sat beside him.

"What is going through your mind?" Trent asked.

"It just doesn't make sense to me," replied Augustus.

"What doesn't?" Trent asked.

"It doesn't make sense that the people he works for," said Augustus, pointing to Jericho, "would want me shot out of the sky. That would be the end of their ability to turn in the lottery ticket."

"What lottery ticket are you talking about?" Trent asked.

Augustus pulled out the winning jackpot lottery ticket, and handed it to him, saying, "This is the Hot Ticket jackpot winner from Iowa. It is worth something like $16 million."

Astonished, Trent said, "No, actually, it is worth $16.5 million."

Augustus gave Trent an inquisitive look.

Trent explained. "I've been hearing about this on the news. The Iowa Lottery folks are waiting for the winner, or winners, to step forward. How did you get this? Did you buy it?"

"I acquired it," said Augustus, taking back the ticket.

He then said, "Apparently, according to what our earless friend here had to say, his organization decided to not continue with their plans of killing me, and my family. Rather, they chose to secure this lottery ticket for a larger payday."

"Well, that is great for you, isn't it?" Trent pressed on. "That means they are not going to kill your family, right?"

"That is the problem," said Augustus. "They, meaning the organization *he* belongs to, are not. However, the people who shot down the helicopter I was in, most likely will."

"Who are they?" Trent asked frantically.

"My former employer," replied Augustus.

Augustus stood up, and looking towards Jericho, said, "I need more information from him, now."

ॐॐॐ

Augustus approached Jericho, saying, "Now that you know I am willing to carve you like a Thanksgiving turkey, you should be prepared to kiss my ass, and give me what I need."

Jonah, while bandaging Jericho, chimed in. "I would not fuck with this guy, so tell him what he needs to know. Besides, I don't have enough dressings to bandage you up if he keeps cutting pieces off you."

"Oh, man, this is not good. I'm all messed up," cried Jericho.

"Not as messed up as you are going to be, if you refuse to help me." Augustus said, brandishing his knife yet again.

Jericho vomited from fear, and cried for mercy.

Augustus stared at Jericho without saying a word.

"Alright, dammit, alright," yelled Jericho. "I'll talk, you goddamned butcher, I'll talk."

"What were you going to do with the ticket?" Augustus demanded. "Where were you taking it? Who were you taking it to?"

"Sugarland, Texas," answered Jericho. "We have a contact there that handles XM finances in the United States. The plan was for the contact to have a lawyer go claim the ticket in Iowa, on XM's behalf."

"How did XM come into possession of this ticket?" Augustus asked.

"They had an operative, a hunter, sent to Iowa to…" Jericho stopped talking, fearful of what Augustus might do to him for finishing that statement.

"I know what he was there for," said Augustus, "keep talking!"

"The hunter came into possession of the lottery ticket during his mission." Jericho said.

"You are saying that part of the hunter's mission was to buy a winning lottery ticket? What the fuck are you talking about? That does not make sense!" Augustus shouted.

"No, he didn't buy it," replied Jericho. "The hunter called XM headquarters when he learned what he had. He reported that he indirectly got the ticket from the personal possessions of two dead United States federal agents."

Augustus flew backwards, as if struck by a bolt of lightning.

"Dios mio," he said aloud, reflecting on the two NSA agents he executed in Iowa. "The agents I killed in Des Moines. It most certainly must be them. I cannot believe that two other federal agents also perished during that operation. It is possible, though, I suppose."

Augustus thought it through further, trying to determine the connection between the dead agents, and the XM operative he found the lottery ticket on outside his mother's home in Iowa. Yet again, he came up with a one-word answer, "Milken."

When I saw Milken with the XM operative at the hospital, that is most likely when Milken gave the order to have my mother killed, and when the lottery ticket changed hands, thought Augustus. *Milken must have been involved with processing the crime scene.*

Augustus walked to Trent.

He then waved Jonah over to them.

When Jonah got there, Augustus said, "I must return to Iowa, immediately. I need this prisoner alive for the foreseeable future. Any thoughts on how I can have that accomplished?"

"I am on it," shouted Jonah.

"Alive," stressed Augustus.

"I know, I know. Trust me, I will keep him alive for as long as you need me to," assured Jonah.

Augustus shifted his focus to Trent.

"I am not saying a word of this to anyone, I can guarantee you that," said Trent.

"The thought didn't even cross my mind," said Augustus, "but good."

"I will help Jonah with whatever he needs," offered Trent.

"No, Mr. Chism, there is no need for you to do that," said Jonah. "I think it is best if you do not take part in any of this. I have got it handled."

Augustus grabbed Trent's shoulder, and said, "Maybe it is time for a much needed, and well-deserved vacation, my friend."

Trent smiled, and said, "I think you are on to something. I will just need to find someone to take care of my precious darlings," referring to his cattle. "You know, they saved my life today. They really are angels from above."

"Just pack and leave, Mr. Chism," Jonah said. "I will take care of them in your absence. I have helped with those beauties of yours plenty of times. I know what needs to be done."

"You already have so much on your plate, Jonah," protested Trent. "I mean, you have the prisoner to mind! That is no small task."

"No, it isn't, that's for sure," agreed Jonah. "But I have an amazing ability at keeping people at bay. Trust me, I have this taken care of!"

"I am a little scared of you right now," Augustus jokingly said to Jonah. "Truthfully, I feel very fortunate to have come across your path, Jonah."

Augustus looked up at the sky, and scanned the land around him. He then sighed loudly, and said, "Okay gentlemen, it is time for me to turn the tables on these bastards, once and for all."

"What is your plan?" Trent asked.

"It is quite simple, really," replied Augustus. "I am going to submit a claim for a winning jackpot lottery ticket."

⌘⌘⌘

SIXTEEN

CAYO ROSARIO, BELIZE

The reverberating sound of an approaching sleek, white speedboat disrupted the serenity of Cayo Rosario, an undeveloped island off the coast of Belize.

Navigating the boat was a local maritime chauffer who knew these shallow waters like the back of his hand.

Standing at the rear of the boat, and holding onto the side railing for balance, was a man wearing wire rimmed glasses, and a light sand linen suit.

The chauffer encircled the tiny island, and parked along the shoreline upon locating the man his passenger was here to meet.

The man in the wire rimmed glasses, and sand linen suit, stepped out of the speedboat. With his pant legs rolled to his knees, he carried his expensive canvas shoes to prevent them from becoming soaked, and waded across the clear blue water to shore.

Rodrigo rose to his feet as the man approached.

"Resun bun," said the man in the wire rimmed glasses, and sand linen suit, in his native language of Garifuna.

"Áhari," said Rodrigo, addressing the man by his name. "It is good to see you. What message do you say you have for me?"

"I received word from our sources in the United States that Jericho, and his team, have been killed. By whom, we do not know. It was a massacre," said Áhari.

"I know that NICO wanted to teach XM a lesson for not honoring our contract with them," said Rodrigo. "However, something tells me, Áhari, that this is something else. They already made their point by shooting down the helicopter. There is no need for them to do this."

"What should I do?" Áhari asked.

"Nothing for now," replied Rodrigo. "I am sure this is not the end of it. We must be prepared for what may come next."

⌘⌘⌘

SEVENTEEN

"When bad men combine, the good must associate; else they will fall one by one, an unpitied sacrifice in a contemptible struggle." - Edmund Burke

DES MOINES, IOWA

Commander Dan Teale of the Iowa State Patrol flipped through the Des Moines radio stations as he drove home from headquarters. Finally, he settled upon a station providing local news updates:

"Thank you, Craig for that traffic report. Our next story is a tragic one, leaving Iowans with many unanswered questions."

"This is a very sad story indeed, Lucas. KBTI has learned from federal officials that the wife and child of former Iowa Safety and Intelligence Bureau Director Augustus Peña were found murdered at an undisclosed location. According to officials with knowledge of the matter, no further information will be disclosed since there is an active investigation into these murders, to include all of the events that led to them."

"My gosh, Jenna. Is there any word on the whereabouts of Augustus Peña?"

"According to the officials I spoke with, Lucas, the whereabouts of Augustus Peña are currently unknown."

"These have been some extremely tense months, Jenna. I know that Iowans have been praying for that family ever since the brutal and brazen attack upon them in West Des Moines. May they rest in peace."

"Absolutely, Lucas. May they rest in peace. In other unrelated news, the Iowa Lottery Commission says that no one has yet to come forward to claim the Hot Ticket lottery jackpot worth $16.5 million dollars…"

Commander Teale turned off the radio.

"Ugh, it seems like all anyone wants to talk about on the news is either the attacks on Augustus Peña's family, or that damn lottery ticket nobody has claimed," he said grumpily. "You would think, after three months, the media could find something else to focus on."

Teale turned onto the highway. Shaking his head, he said, "I might as well entertain myself instead," and began singing his favorite country songs. By the time Commander Teale arrived home, his crooning had morphed into enthusiastic whistling.

Teale parked his car in the garage, and entered his house.

On the kitchen table was a note from his wife. She wanted him to know that she was staying overnight with her sister in Marion, Iowa, and that supper was in the refrigerator.

Teale retrieved his dinner, warmed it in the microwave, and returned to the kitchen table to eat.

As he ate, he noticed an extra note on the table that was not there moments ago.

Alarmed, Commander Teale slowly reached for it, while glancing towards his service weapon, which was hanging in its holster on his coat tree.

෧෧෧

In neat, cursive letters, the extra note on the kitchen table read:

> *"When I speak, do not move. I am not here to kill you, but I will, if I have no choice."*

Commander Teale returned the note to the table, and said - "Okay, you have my attention. Who are you, and what do you want?"

"I want you to save my former deputy director from certain death. I also need you to help me piece together some loose ends."

"Director Peña, is that you?"

"Former Director Peña," Augustus sadly replied.

"Can I turn to look at you?" Teale asked.

"Can I trust that you are not going to make an attempt at arresting me?" Augustus answered.

"I have no clear thoughts on all that occurred that day, Mr. Peña. So, no, I am not going to arrest you. Besides, the feds have assumed jurisdiction over this matter. Quite frankly, it would be too much paperwork for me to arrest you, and hand you over to them."

"You can turn to face me," said Augustus.

Commander Teale turned slowly, and observed Augustus sitting in the shadows.

"I heard about your wife and son on my way home tonight. I have no words." Teale said.

"I learned about it shortly after it occurred. I did not believe it…did not want to believe it. But yes, it is true. You have no words because no words exist that can speak to all that has happened." Augustus said.

"What did happen to you and your family that day?" Teale asked, referring to the dreadful day in December when NICO assassins unsuccessfully attempted to wipe out Augustus and his family during multiple attacks.

"The only way for me to answer your question, is to be very blunt with you about my background." Augustus replied.

"Okay, that's fine with me. I'm all ears." Teale said.

"I was once an assassin for the United States government. I was not a contractor. I was a federal employee. I will spare you the details, but, at some point, my former employer decided that I was too much of a political liability to remain alive."

"I guess I can understand the twisted logic there, but, what about your family?" Teale queried.

"I have obsessed over that very same question, commander. I believe that the decision to kill my family was ultimately nothing more than a tactical option employed by the initial perpetrator. When that was unsuccessful, it seemingly spiraled out of control, and was incorporated into the greater plan to assassinate me."

"I'm sorry, I need some help with this. You refer to the decision to murder your family as a tactical option, Mr. Peña. Who makes those types of tactical decisions?" Teale pressed.

"Professional killers, Commander Teale, that's who." Augustus replied.

"Look, Director - "

"Mister, please," insisted Augustus.

"Mister Peña. I possess zero insight into the world you have just presented to me. Consequently, I do not know how in blazes I can help you."

"Perhaps you do not have insight," said Augustus, "but you do have a moral compass. Nothing that occurred that day feels right to you, correct?"

"That doesn't matter," Teale replied.

"Of course, it matters Commander Teale, of course it does. Your many years of law enforcement experience tells you that something is amiss. I know it does." Augustus hammered.

"What is it that you think I know, Mr. Peña?" Teale pleaded. "Give me one solid item that you think I have knowledge of that is directly related to your predicament."

"I can do better than that, Commander Teale," said Augustus. "I can give you 16.5 million items that you can assist me with."

કે કે કે

Commander Teale frowned, saying, "What in God's green earth are you talking about, Mr. Peña?"

Augustus leaned towards Teale, and spoke softly. "The winning jackpot lottery ticket. The one that is all over the news, and the one I have in my possession."

Commander Teale looked incredulously at Augustus, and said, "Good heavens, you didn't just say a winning jackpot lottery ticket, did you?"

"You bet your ass I did," replied Augustus, "and it is worth sixteen and a half million dollars. In fact, it is worth more than the price of the contract on my head. This whole scheme to assassinate me is a bit convoluted, and involves more than one entity, to include contracted killers. From what I have learned, the contractors decided that this piece of paper is more valuable to them than fulfilling their contractual obligation of taking my life."

Augustus produced the lottery ticket, and handed it to Commander Teale, saying, "Can you help me figure out who bought this ticket?"

"I'll be damned. Just when I thought things were somewhat getting back to normal," muttered Teale.

Augustus continued. "I came into possession of this ticket by way of a contracted killer."

Commander Teale tilted his head, expressing a curious look on his face, signifying his confusion.

"I killed a man, Commander Teale, who had been sent to kill my mother. He was outside her house when I located him. After I killed him, I searched his body, and he had this ticket on him. Prior to that encounter, I saw this man with my former boss. My former boss is an NSA program director. However, he was most likely posing as a Department of Justice or Homeland Security official, to conceal NSA's involvement."

Commander Teale was about to refute the validity of Augustus' claims. Suddenly, a memory came to mind. It was of him speaking with an agent from the U.S. Department of Homeland Security. The agent had spoken of recently purchasing a lottery ticket.

"What date was the ticket purchased?" Teale asked.

"December 23rd," replied Augustus.

Commander Teale struggled for a moment, before saying, "I might know of someone from the federal government that bought a lottery ticket that day."

"I don't care if some random public servant bought a lottery ticket that day," Augustus shot back.

"Not some random public servant," Teale responded, "but an agent from the U.S. Department of Homeland Security who was in town to specifically work your case."

"Do you have a description of what the agent looks like?" Augustus asked.

"I can tell you what he looked like. The agent was subsequently murdered. In fact, word on the wire is that you killed him, Mr. Peña. Well, both he and his partner were killed," Teale clarified.

"Describe the agent's physical characteristics to me," demanded Augustus.

"He was young, and from the East Coast. His partner was older -"

"The younger agent," pressed Augustus, "was he black? Was he an African American?"

"Yes," replied Teale.

"And his partner, an older white male, correct?" Augustus quickly followed up.

"That is also correct," replied Teale, looking at Augustus suspiciously.

"There is no need for you to speculate further," said Augustus. "Yes, I killed them both."

Commander Teale sat stone cold silent. He seemed paralyzed from shock.

Augustus continued with his narrative. "They were both NSA field operatives, Commander Teale, not law enforcement agents. The fact of the matter is they were assassins, sent to clean up a sub-agency program mess - me."

"I am struggling to understand how it is that the lottery ticket ended up in your possession," said Teale.

"So am I," said Augustus, as he stood up, and retrieved the ticket from Teale. "However, the information you provided is very helpful for me to figure it out."

Shifting his focus, Augustus worriedly asked, "Is Molander okay?"

"Chad Molander has been in federal protective custody from the moment he was located unconscious in that bunker-like facility," said Teale. "Jesus. Who knew such a place existed right here in Des Moines, Iowa? Anyway, as I understand it, he is back in the hospital for a couple of days, undergoing follow-up treatment. Apparently, he had some sort of neurological reaction to whatever concoction he injected himself with to knock himself out during that fiasco."

"I see," whispered Augustus, feeling sheepish for having prepared the injection that rendered Chad unconscious while Augustus, his family, and Doctor Broderson evacuated the underground installation codenamed The Station.

Commander Teale changed the subject. "I don't know how they are able to get away with all of this," he protested, visibly distraught.

"They get away with it," said Augustus, "because nobody knows what is going on. In the unlikely event someone does manage to figure it out, they are either dismissed as a lunatic, labeled a conspiracy theorist, or simply killed."

"What are you planning on doing, Mr. Peña?"

"Exposure shall be my revenge, Commander Teale. Sunlight is the best sanitizer, and that is exactly what I will provide to our country, being the dedicated public servant that I am. I do not know whether my actions will make me a patriot, or a traitor. What I do know, is that this is what needs to be done."

"Maybe it makes you a little bit of both," suggested Teale.

"Perhaps," agreed Augustus. "But before I do this, it is of vital importance that I get my mother, and Chad Molander, to safety. The NSA is going to kill them, Commander Teale. There is no doubt about it. I will handle my mother's safety. But you need to get Molander somewhere far off the grid, so that his whereabouts cannot be traced."

"How exactly do I do that?" Teale asked.

"You said that Molander is at the hospital for a few days," replied Augustus. "I would go there at once. Every second counts. Do not delay. I have faith that you will figure it out once you get there."

As Augustus exited Teale's home, he said, "Save Chad's life, commander. He represents the best, and brightest, of our nation's future."

࿇ ࿇ ࿇

Commander Teale sat in silence for what felt like hours. He struggled with shaking off the jolt from hearing Augustus' confession to killing the two federal agents.

He had long suspected Augustus' involvement in the murders, but he possessed no proof.

The cameras that should have recorded their slayings had mysteriously malfunctioned, rendered useless by a powerful computer virus.

When Commander Teale inquired into any backup recordings that may exist, federal authorities informed him that the virus decimated all recordings, in addition to the cameras themselves.

Moreover, the only person to survive that horrific scene was Trooper Paul Hoffmeyer. However, he was unable to communicate with anyone about how exactly those two agents died. Shortly after the incident, Hoffmeyer suffered a massive stroke, presumably from the injuries he sustained. The stroke was so severe that he fell into a coma, from which he had yet to emerge.

Until now, Commander Teale could only rely on his gut, and pure speculation, as to what occurred on that fateful day; about who killed those two agents, and about who injured Trooper Hoffmeyer so gravely.

"There is no more mystery to it," said Teale. "Peña is up to his ears in problems. He seems to have his hands in practically every strange occurrence that has come up over the past several months."

Teale stood up, and leaned over the kitchen counter. "How in the hell a lottery ticket became a part of this, I will never understand. But the truth is stranger than fiction, I guess."

Commander Teale walked to the coat tree, and put on his holster, saying, "I had better get Chad Molander to a safe place. I have no doubt that Peña knows what he is talking about."

He then rushed to the hospital to save Chad Molander from imminent doom.

⌘⌘⌘

EIGHTEEN

Deputy Special Agent in Charge (DSAC) David Wilkerson had been tasked by the F.B.I. as the operational manager for the Augustus Peña matter.

Having recently arrived in Iowa, DSAC Wilkerson was busy settling into his temporary office, located within the Des Moines federal building.

Angered by the agency IT department's failure to have his network connections up and running, DSAC Wilkerson lashed out upon hearing a knock on his office door.

"What do you want?" he barked.

The door opened, and his mission support specialist, Juanita, entered. She then said, "DSAC Wilkerson, the individual from Coast Guard Investigative Services (CGIS) is here. Are you ready to meet with him?"

"Well, now is as good a time as any since I cannot get crap done around here. Send him in, and be sure to call IT to tell them how pissed off I am at their incompetence!" DSAC Wilkerson replied.

"Absolutely sir," Juanita said, exiting his office.

Seconds later a tall, older man appeared in the doorway wearing civilian attire. The two men made brief eye contact, sizing each other up, and then smiled at each other.

"Holy mother of God," said DSAC Wilkerson. "CGIS must be in a really bad way, scraping the bottom of the pot like this. They really did send your old, sorry ass to do this!"

"I may be old," replied the man from CGIS, "but I can still sweep the sidewalk with you eight days a week."

"And...I see that you are still as dumb as a tent full of ass clowns," retorted DSAC Wilkerson.

The two men bellowed with laughter, and then slammed into each other as they hugged, knocking a few items from DSAC Wilkerson's desk onto the floor.

"You look great!" DSAC Wilkerson said. "How is the cancer? Based on what I had heard through the grapevine, I thought it got pretty bad."

The office door opened, and Juanita entered. "Is everything okay, sir?" She asked. "I heard a lot of noise in here."

DSAC Wilkerson laughed, saying, "This here is CGIS Chief Warrant Officer Patrick Humphries. He is going to be my eyes and ears during this operation. I need someone I can trust, someone that I have worked with extensively. This man and I go way back conducting cross-agency investigations, and he is the perfect fit. Be sure he has all that he needs, to include a freaking network connection for Christ's sake."

Turning to Chief Warrant Officer Humphries, DSAC Wilkerson asked, "Seriously, though. You are not going to die on me out there, are you?"

"I may not have long to go," Chief Humphries replied half-jokingly, "but I owed you quite a bit, and I plan on going out in style."

ೲೲೲ

It was a crisp Iowa evening as CGIS Chief Warrant Officer Patrick Humphries drove to his destination. Looking at his vehicle's GPS unit, he said to himself, "It should be around the next corner."

However, upon making a left turn at the corner, he realized he did not need the GPS unit to identify the house.

The driveway of his destination, a modest Tudor style house, was lined with black SUVs, while several Federal Protective Service (FPS) agents stood guard throughout the property.

Chief Humphries turned into the driveway, and stopped when prompted to do so by an agent. Lowering his driver-side window, he handed the FPS agent his badged credentials.

"I am Chief Warrant Officer Patrick Humphries with Coast Guard Investigative Service. DSAC Wilkerson has directed me to check in on the protectee, and to assess the security apparatus in place."

The FPS agent returned Chief Humphries his credentials, and said, "The DSAC informed us you would be arriving soon, and to provide you with full cooperation. Welcome, Chief. You can pull up alongside the vehicle closest to the house."

Chief Humphries parked his car, and exited. Waiting for him were two FPS agents.

"Chief Humphries, I presume," said one of the agents, reaching out for a handshake.

"You got it," replied Chief Humphries.

"Welcome on station. I am FPS Agent Morelli, and this is FPS Agent Lewis. We are here to assist you with whatever you need."

"Thank you," replied Chief Humphries. He then asked, "What is the status of the protectee? Have there been any attempted security breaches?"

"Other than an occasional news reporter or two snooping around, it has been pretty tight, with zero incidents to report," replied FPS Agent Morelli.

FPS Agent Lewis chimed in, saying, "The biggest action we have had was from the protectee."

"What do you mean?" Chief Humphries asked.

"The protectee threw us all out of the house. She put up one hell of a fight, too, let me tell you," FPS Agent Lewis replied.

"Yeah," said FPS Agent Morelli, laughing. "She even pulled out a switchblade knife, from who knows where, and threatened to cut off our private parts if we did not get the eff out of her house!"

Chief Humphries cried out with laughter, and said, "The apple most definitely did not fall far from that tree. This is exactly what I would expect from the mother of Augustus Peña."

Scanning the brightly lit property, Chief Humphries said, "Listen, fellas. I am going to take a different approach here. I need to get in there, and check on her. It is what I am here to do under direct orders. My plan is to go in there alone. However, I am pretty darn certain she is a bit intimidated, and overwhelmed, by your large presence out here. It would really help me out if you, and your men, take leave from here. Not for long, maybe, say, thirty to forty minutes. That will put her at ease, I am sure of it. This will provide me with the best possible opportunity at completing the task DSAC Wilkerson has assigned me. It may also save me from having my balls cut off."

FPS Agent Morelli thought for a moment, and said, "Under normal circumstances I would not leave my post. However, these are not normal circumstances. Not at all," he chuckled. "The team can use a quick break. The last few months have exhausted us all."

FPS Agent Lewis then said, "The surrounding area is loaded with food joints. We won't be more than five minutes away if you need us."

"That sounds perfect," replied Chief Humphries. "I would like to enter the house through the garage. Can you open it for me?"

"Sure thing," replied FPS Agent Morelli. "Here is the new master key for the house," he said, handing it to Chief Humphries.

The garage door opened. Chief Humphries thanked the FPS agents, and pulled his car inside.

ॐ ॐ ॐ

Chief Humphries parked his government sedan in the garage. Upon exiting the vehicle, he closed the garage door by pushing an electronic pad located next to the door that led into the house.

Once the garage door fully closed, Chief Humphries walked to the trunk of his car, and opened it.

"That worked like a freaking charm," Augustus said from inside the trunk. "Now help me get out of here."

"It sure did," Chief Humphries replied. "But we have maybe twenty to twenty-five minutes to work with to get your mother out of here, undetected."

Unbeknownst to DSAC Wilkerson, Chief Humphries, a local area resident, had developed a strong personal relationship with Augustus over the past several years. The two men met at a local watering hole, where they bitched about their jobs, politics, and whatever else came to mind. It did not take long before the duo spent countless hours playing horrible rounds of golf together, while continuing their relentless bitching sessions over gallons of cheap beer.

Also unbeknownst to DSAC Wilkerson was the fact that Chief Humphries knew of a past sexual affair between DSAC Wilkerson, and his ex-wife. Chief Humphries learned of the affair by monitoring his wife's electronic communications after he became suspicious. Although furious at his wife for engaging in an extramarital affair, he never brought it up with her, and the marriage quietly dissolved.

Chief Humphries' knowledge of this affair never made its way back to DSAC Wilkerson, making him ignorant of Chief Humphries' insatiable desire for revenge.

As fate would have it, Chief Humphries received a call from CGIS headquarters directing him to assist DSAC Wilkerson, just as Augustus finished explaining to him all that had happened.

After completing the phone call with CGIS headquarters, Chief Humphries said to Augustus, "What you have experienced, my dear friend, is unimaginable. As you know, I am dying of cancer, and am limited with what I can do for you. However, I have just been provided an opportunity to not only seek the revenge I so much desire, but to also present a Terminal Gift from me, to you."

Now, in the garage, Chief Humphries helped Augustus get out of the car's trunk.

"This is your last opportunity to back out of this," Augustus said.

Chief Humphries replied, "Kiss my ass, and get inside the house!"

જ્જ્જ્

The interior of the house was dark, and humid. It was exactly the way Noemi Peña, Augustus' mother, liked it.

It was also tranquil. There was no radio, or television playing.

Noemi Peña loved to watch Spanish-language soap opera programs if she were not listening to news broadcasts on the radio. Something was almost always playing in the background. The lack of sound worried Augustus. His mother was not known to go to bed early. For as long as he could remember, she did not go to sleep until close to midnight.

In the dimly lit hallway, Chief Humphries observed a sense of concern emanate across Augustus' face.

Augustus was about to call out for his mother when Chief Humphries bumped into a floor lamp. The lamp had colorful strings of beads dangling all around it. The beads made a loud, swarming sound that echoed throughout the hallway, as they banged together from the contact.

Instantly, the sounds of the beads crashing together were muted by the crackling recoil sounds of Noemi Peña's lever action .30-30 Winchester rifle.

One of the rounds struck Chief Humphries square in the chest. He fell hard onto the floor.

One of the rounds smashed into the wall behind Augustus. The shot missed his head by a fraction of an inch.

"Hijos de la gran puta, desgraciados!" Noemi Peña cursed in her native Puerto Rican dialect of Spanish. "Te voy a matar!" She screamed, informing her targets of their impending death, at her hands, as she emptied her weapon.

Augustus screamed when his mother stopped to reload her Winchester, "Mom, it's me, Augustino. Stop shooting! Stop shooting!"

Noemi recognized her son's voice, and threw her weapon to the floor.

Augustus ran to Chief Humphries to assess his wound.

Chief Humphries was groggy. His speech was slightly slurred when he said, "Oh, shit…your mother is an amazing shot with that thing."

Augustus did not see blood on Chief Humphries. He tore open the Chief's shirt, and sighed when he saw the bulletproof vest that just saved his friend's life.

"Mira, is he dead? Did I kill him?" Noemi asked when she arrived by their side.

"Diablo, ma. No, you didn't kill him. His is wearing a vest. Where did you get that thing?" Augustus demanded.

"Ah, no te importa. Don't worry about it, hijo," replied Noemi. "You are not the only one in the family that loves weapons, you know."

Augustus and Chief Humphries shook their heads in disbelief.

Chief Humphries started to laugh, but coughed from pain instead. He then said, "We need to hurry up. We do not have much time before the security detail returns."

"Where are we going?" Noemi asked.

"I am taking you to Nathaniel," replied Augustus.

"But the news said that he, and Jennifer, have been killed," said Noemi.

"Jennifer is dead, ma. These animals killed her, and they wanted to kill Nathaniel too, but he is safe. The thing is, ma, that for Nathaniel to remain alive, everyone must believe he died with his mother."

Noemi sprung onto Augustus and cried out, "Gracias a Dios," thanking God for sparing the life of her grandson.

She then wiped away her tears, and said, "I am bringing my Winchester."

⌘⌘⌘

NINETEEN

It was 11 p.m., and Commander Dan Teale tried his best to refrain from speeding along the narrow Des Moines city streets.

Driving his neighbor's car to avoid detection, he said, "Getting pulled over for speeding, and revealing my identity at this juncture, would not aid in my need to travel clandestinely. I feel wary of who I can trust. I must be as inconspicuous as possible."

Commander Teale nervously tapped the steering wheel. He then said, "Anything I do to attract attention will certainly draw the ire of whoever is hunting Peña."

The commander pulled into the hospital parking lot, which was nearly full. He had not expected this many vehicles. Finding a space to park seemed impossible. Finally, he located a spot towards the rear of the lot, and parked the car.

"What am I doing?" Commander Teale growled. "I am not a goddamn spy. I have no idea what I am doing. I could have already given myself away for all I know."

Commander Teale exited his vehicle. He then visually scanned the area around him for suspicious activity.

Convinced that he saw no danger, the commander strode to the hospital's main entrance.

Although he thoroughly scanned the area, Commander Teale failed to notice a late model van parked several rows away.

It had blacked out windows, and its engine was running.

ॐॐॐ

Commander Teale entered the hospital through its main entrance.

Reality suddenly set in, and the commander understood that no matter how inconspicuous he wanted to be, he simply could not operate clandestinely in this environment.

Commander Teale searched for a familiar face amongst the crowd of mostly federal law enforcement personnel.

This place is crawling with feds, he thought. *I must stick out like a sore thumb.*

He was not entirely certain he could trust anyone he recognized. Nevertheless, a familiar face would make him feel more at ease.

Commander Teale had a paranoid sense that, although he was unable to recognize the agents, his identity was readily apparent to them.

Why did I drive my neighbor's car? he thought. *It makes no damn bit of difference. Also, what is it that I think I am going to accomplish here? I have no plan on how to save Chad Molander. I am doomed.*

ॐॐॐ

Outside, the older model van with blacked out windows crept across the hospital parking lot. Like an apex predator on the hunt, the van lurked purposefully towards its quarry.

The van stopped.

It then slowly backed up into the open parking spot next to where Commander Teale parked his neighbor's car.

ॐॐॐ

Commander Teale snapped out of it. Shaking off his concerns, he pressed forward with his mission. He sighed, and sought someone to speak with.

A man standing by the main set of elevators waved at him.

Commander Teale did not recognize the man, but went to him anyway.

"Good evening," Commander Teale greeted, as he handed the man his badged credentials.

The man did not bother inspecting the credentials, and said, "Commander Dan Teale. Good evening. I have been expecting you."

Commander Teale stiffened. "I was not notified I would be expected here," he said to the man. "I simply came by to…"

The man interrupted him. "Commander, my name is Patrick Humphries. I am a Chief Warrant Officer with CGIS, Coast Guard Investigative Service."

Commander Teale bellowed, "The Coast Guard? What in the name of all that is good is the Coast Guard doing here? More importantly, why would you be expecting me?"

Chief Humphries squeezed Commander Teale's shoulder, and whispered into his ear, "I am an old friend of Augustus Peña." He locked eyes with Commander Teale, nodding his head in a manner suggesting they were on the same mission.

Commander Teale did not know what to do with this information. Nevertheless, he felt relieved that he apparently was not doing this by himself.

"Come with me," Chief Humphries said to the commander. "We need to get this done immediately. This place is crawling with NSA agents. Not to mention, there are rumors of international bounty hunters heading this way…to pick up on Augustus Peña's trail."

"How do we survive this?" Commander Teale queried.

"I don't know that we do," Chief Humphries replied bluntly. "But we do all that we can, and go out with dignity."

"We are on a suicide mission!" Commander Teale growled. "Augustus Peña sat in my living room, he fed me a load of horse shit, and sent me on a suicide mission!"

Chief Humphries chuckled. "You are calling this a suicide mission? Commander, you were already dead when Augustus got to you."

"I do not understand what you are saying to me," Commander Teale said.

"Check your phone, commander," replied Chief Humphries. "I am assuming that you placed it into silent mode, because I have not heard it ring."

Commander Teale removed his phone from his belt clip. He squinted his eyes, and furrowed his brows.

The screen on his mobile phone showed that he missed ten calls, and another one was coming through.

⤙⤙⤙

A chill rushed through Commander Teale's body as he answered his phone.

"Sir. Oh, thank goodness," the voice on the other end of the call said excitedly.

The caller then yelled to other people, saying, "I got him! I have Commander Teale on the phone!"

"Sir, are you still there?" The caller asked nervously.

"I am. Who is this? What is going on? What is this about?" Commander Teale demanded.

"This is Detective Peck with the Des Moines Police Department. Our units responded to an anonymous call regarding suspicious activity around your home. The caller thought it was possibly a home invasion."

Commander Teale immediately dismissed the potential of any danger. He figured that the tipster must have called after witnessing Augustus sneak into his home.

That notion quickly vanished.

"When the units arrived at your home," continued Detective Peck, "they observed a light flickering from what appeared to be your basement. Consequently, they approached your egress window, and peered inside."

"What did they see?" Commander Teale asked.

"They observed, and I confirmed after arriving on scene, four deceased individuals. Commander, they were all stacked on top of each other."

"WHAT?" Commander Teale screamed.

"There's more, sir," replied Detective Peck. "The individuals all wore black military-styled clothing, and they were armed as if they were invading Iraq."

"My God," Commander Teale said. "Have you identified them?"

"Negative, sir. The only thing I can positively report is that the assailants were comprised of three males, and one female."

"How were they killed?" Commander Teale pressed.

"That's the thing, sir," replied Detective Peck. "Based on their attire, and equipment, the deceased appear to have been professionals. However, whoever killed them was more proficient than they were."

"Why do you say that?" Commander Teale queried.

"They were all stabbed to death. Each of the deceased had puncture wounds to their neck, and armpit areas. Although forensics has yet to provide their final assessment, it was obvious that the killer knew their craft very well, and ended them quickly."

"The wounds do not necessarily suggest they were killed quickly, do they Detective?" countered Teale.

"No, they don't, sir," agreed Detective Peck. "However, there is something else which suggests that they were."

"And what would that be?" Commander Teale asked.

"None of the assailants had defensive wounds, suggesting they didn't see it coming. Moreover, none of them got to fire a single round from their weapons, and each of their safety catches were switched off. The weapons were hot, sir, yet they did not fire a shot."

Detective Peck then briefed Commander Teale on the status of his wife, and Commander Teale dropped the phone onto the floor.

"Oh, Jesus. Please no," Commander Teale exclaimed. He then looked at Chief Humphries with an expression of horror.

"They were a hit squad," said Chief Humphries, flatly. "You apparently asked too many questions, and started digging too deep. Augustus and I arrived at your home shortly after they did. Unfortunately, they had already murdered your wife."

Commander Teale fell to his knees, and almost vomited.

"Augustus executed them, commander, and placed them in your basement." Chief Humphries continued.

"Where is my wife?" Commander Teale sobbingly asked.

"Augustus placed her in her bed. She is resting peacefully, commander. There is no time for you to go back and address this. Nor is it safe for you to do so. That would be a true suicide mission, commander."

Commander Teale asked, "What about the anonymous tipster who called in the suspicious activity?"

"Augustus called the police after you left your home to come here."

"Why did he do that?" Commander Teale asked.

"It is part of Augustus' campaign of exposure. There will be no more secrets. All will be revealed in due course," Chief Humphries replied.

"Where is Augustus now?" Commander Teale asked.

Chief Humphries replied, "We recovered his mother earlier this evening, Commander Teale. Although Augustus did not share the exact details of his plan, I assume he is taking her to safety."

"Why are you helping him?" Commander Teale asked.

"As I said," replied Chief Humphries. "Augustus and I are old friends. I always said that I would bet my life on that man, which is what I am doing right now."

Chief Humphries looked Commander Teale in the eyes, and said, "It is time to move, commander. It is now, or never."

⌘⌘⌘

TWENTY

The mere thought of his wife's murder made Commander Teale feel faint. All he wanted to do was bolt from the hospital, and run to his dead wife's side. He wanted to disappear forever.

However, Commander Teale knew that breaking down, and fading away into the ether was not an acceptable choice.

"I have the rest of my life to properly mourn the loss of the only woman I ever loved," he sobbed. "What I need to focus on right now, at this moment in time, is to end this barbaric bloodshed."

Commander Teale was proud to call himself a native Iowan. To him, this meant more than a place. It meant hard work, a determination to succeed, and an unwavering moral compass.

But it also meant something else. "Accountability," he said, wiping away tears.

Having earned a reputation for being an honorable, and committed law enforcement professional, his words commanded action, and he knew it.

"First the Peña family, then mine. Who knows how many other deaths and horrific acts occurred in between those?" Commander Teale uttered. "Toss in a jackpot lottery ticket that already has blood on it, and we have a lot of people who need to be held accountable."

Commander Teale looked towards Chief Humphries, and said, "But first, I need to help that man save Chad Molander. Enough is enough, and I simply will not have any more of it."

ล้ล้ล้

With Commander Teale by his side, Chief Humphries approached a law enforcement officer (LEO) who was speaking into his two-way radio, while directing personnel using arm gestures.

Chief Humphries introduced himself, and asked, "Are you in charge of this site?"

Agitated, the LEO glared at Chief Humphries. He then tipped his police uniform hat, saying, "Of course not. I am not that high up the chain of command, or are you not able to see that?"

Ignoring the LEO's rude response, Chief Humphries said, "I need to speak with the COG, immediately. There is a dire emergency developing which requires deconfliction."

The LEO stared at Chief Humphries with a confused look.

"Seriously, you do not know what COG means?" Chief Humphries mocked. "Commander on the Ground, man. I need to coordinate with the COG, right now."

The LEO was about to retort when his two-way radio squelched.

"Oh, look, smartass," the LEO said. "It's the COG on the radio. I will put you through to him. Would you like for me to go get you some coffee? Perhaps a warm sandwich as well, to help make you comfortable?"

"Cut the shit," Chief Humphries shot back. "Get me on that radio."

The LEO rolled his eyes, then spoke into the radio. "Top, I have a Chief Warrant Officer here from Coast Guard Investigative Service. He is accompanied by…I'm sorry, pal. Who are you again?"

Commander Teale identified himself.

The LEO continued speaking into the two-way radio. "Oh right, yeah. He is accompanied by Commander Dan Teale of the Iowa State Patrol. The Chief here says there is an emergency developing that requires your assistance. According to the paperwork he showed me, it appears that he is here under orders from DSAC Wilkerson."

The LEO nodded as he listened to the COG's response, then said, "Copy that, sir. I will escort them up momentarily."

২৯ ২৯ ২৯

The LEO escorted them to the hospital's second floor, where the COG was set up for this operation.

"Right through those swinging doors is where you both want to go," the LEO said, pointing. "Top, um, I mean, the COG is expecting you."

Chief Humphries, and Commander Teale, parted ways with the LEO, and moved through the swinging doors.

"Gentlemen," the COG said as they entered. "Welcome. Please have a seat."

"Sir," Chief Humphries began.

"Mason, please," replied the COG, waving his hand as he spoke. "Just call me Mason."

"Mason, we have an urgent matter to discuss with you regarding…" Chief Humphries began saying.

"I want to apologize outright," said COG Mason. "I am prone to interrupting people when I have a good idea what they are about to say."

Chief Humphries became visibly agitated, and Commander Teale was about to speak, when COG Mason handed them each a faxed document.

"I am sorry for your loss, Commander Teale," COG Mason said. "This notification is just now being pushed out to all law enforcement command posts nationwide. I imagine that your presence here, as opposed to you being by your wife's side, means we have a crisis on our hands."

Looking at Chief Humphries, COG Mason said, "I contacted DSAC Wilkerson as you were being escorted up here. It is my understanding I am to provide you with whatever assistance you may require."

Relieved, Chief Humphries replied, "The protectee, Chad Molander, must be relocated at once. The attack against Commander Teale's wife is a continuation of this whole Augustus Peña shitshow. I am prepared to personally move Molander to a secure location. The situation is fluid, the secure location is not known to me at this time, but I must move, now."

"What do you need?" Mason asked.

"An inconspicuous way out of this hospital with Molander," Chief Humphries replied.

৵৵৵

Chief Humphries coughed, and gasped for air as he hurriedly pushed Chad Molander's wheelchair along the hospital's main floor corridor.

Molander was lucid, but did not question what was happening. Recognizing Chief Humphries as a friend of his former boss, Molander nodded at him, and smiled. To Molander, it was reminiscent of the day of the attacks against the Peña family, making him appreciate the current sense of urgency.

COG Mason provided Chief Humphries with an inconspicuous exit from the hospital, clearing a pathway to a loading dock area at the rear of the hospital.

Chief Humphries stopped just short of the loading dock's opening. "I hope the commander gets here soon," he said aloud, touching his chest. "I am not doing very well."

A set of headlights appeared from a vehicle that turned onto the roadway which led to the loading dock.

Chief Humphries patted Chad Molander on the shoulder, saying, "Get ready, son. Here he comes."

ॐॐॐ

Commander Teale hustled across the hospital parking lot. Reaching into his pocket for the car key, he thought, *I am certain that when good old Mr. Wicket asked me to take care of his roomy, expensive car while he traveled throughout Europe, he did not expect for me to use it to smuggle someone to safety.*

An overwhelming sadness over his wife's murder began to take hold of him. "Stop it!" Commander Teale shouted. "I need to keep a clear head, and get this done." Struggling to focus, he fumbled the car key as he tried to open his neighbor's car.

This lack of focus prevented the commander from noticing the older model van with blacked out windows, and a slightly opened side door, parked next to him.

Commander Teale opened his neighbor's car door, and was instantly slammed over his head from behind with a helmet. He was then dragged into the van.

⌘⌘⌘

TWENTY-ONE

The force of the helmet crashing over Commander Teale's head caused him to bleed. He was disoriented, and in great pain.

"What is this?" Commander Teale asked in a weak voice.

The shrill sound of speakers turning on rattled the commander's brain, adding a massive headache to his agony.

Finally, the harsh sounds stopped, and NSA Director Frank Newberry began speaking. "You have been very busy investigating the Augustus Peña matter, haven't you Commander Dan Teale of the Iowa State Patrol?"

"What in the…" Commander Teale barked. He was soon silenced by a punch to his stomach from the NSA agent who pulled him into the van.

Newberry continued, "My guy next to you, commander, is patched into our conversation. If you speak without being told to, he will correct your behavior."

Commander Teale nodded in acknowledgment of Newberry's words.

"It looks like he understands, sir," the NSA agent said to Newberry.

"Fantastic," Newberry replied, then saying, "You, commander, have been probing deeply into matters that some would argue are beyond your jurisdictional reach. Why is that?"

"I have no idea what –," Commander Teale shouted before another punch to his gut silenced him.

"Oh, now, come on," Newbery pressed. "We know that in addition to your curiosity about the malfunctioning of citywide cameras the day of the Peña attacks, you have been corresponding with members of the congressional intelligence committee in charge of oversight regarding the underground installation in Des Moines, codenamed, The Station."

Commander Teale snorted, but did not respond.

"You have also been snooping around other jurisdictions," said Newberry, "to determine if an installation like The Station exists within their respective borders. Thankfully for us, your miscreant neighbors to the north are as corrupt as an Afghan village elder, and leak like a sieve. They are always eager to receive large payments of cash in return for leaked intelligence. God bless the crooked State of Minnesota."

"Sir," the NSA agent said to Newberry. "Shall I begin to drive?"

"Yes, you shall," Newberry answered. "Go to the loading dock at the rear of the hospital."

Shifting his focus, Newberry mockingly said, "You see, Commander Dan Teale of the Iowa State Patrol, I possess a wealth of knowledge that manifests from numerous sources at all levels of government. Sources who, quite frankly, cannot walk away from the temptation of revealing juicy bits of information. In case you are wondering, commander, the answer is yes. I do know that our target, Mr. Chad Molander, is at the loading dock awaiting evacuation."

Commander Teale thrashed about in anger, shouting obscenities at the top of his lungs as the NSA agent started to drive the van.

꙲꙲꙲

Frank Newberry ended the communication by saying to Commander Teale, "I will dispose of you, and Mr. Molander, after I learn exactly what it is that you both know, and who you both have shared that information with."

The NSA agent turned the van onto the driveway that led to the hospital's loading dock area.

Commander Teale never felt so helpless in his life. He was immobilized, and unable to put up a fight. To make matters worse, he was blinded by the contraption over his head, which prevented him from looking at his tormentor in the eyes.

"What a pathetic way to go out," Commander Teale said. "Please, God. You did not spare my wife's life, and I do not ask for you to spare mine. What I do ask of you, Lord, is that you spare the life of Chad Molander, and that you stop these demons in their tracks."

The van's engine growled lowly as it slowed down, eventually stopping alongside the loading dock.

The loading dock was empty.

The NSA agent flashed his headlights several times, hoping that doing so would produce a response from within. He smirked upon seeing Chief Humphries appear at the loading dock, pushing a wheelchair.

The NSA agent made his way to the middle of the van's cabin, and grabbed his M-4 carbine rifle.

After checking to make sure the weapon was ready to fire, the NSA agent slid open the van's side door, and jumped outside.

જન્જન્જન્

Standing just beyond the van, the NSA agent raised his weapon, and said, "Step away from the wheelchair. I am a federal agent, and I am taking this man into custody as a matter of national security."

Chief Humphries refused to comply.

The NSA agent had a clear shot at Chief Humphries. He was about to squeeze the trigger when his right thigh stung with a red-hot pain.

The NSA agent retracted his finger from the trigger, and looked down at his thigh.

He saw blood spurting from it onto the ground, indicating that his femoral artery had been severed.

Suddenly, he experienced the same pain in his left thigh.

Unable to stand, the NSA agent dropped onto his knees, as Augustus Peña grabbed ahold of his head, and slit his throat.

જન્જન્જન્

Augustus removed Chad Molander from his wheelchair. He then fireman-carried his former Iowa Safety and Intelligence Bureau deputy director to the van.

Next, Augustus removed the helmet from a wildly confused Commander Teale, and tossed it aside.

Looking at the dead man on the ground, Augustus said, "That man was an NSA assassin, and he needed to die."

Augustus jumped into the van's driver's seat saying, "We have maybe one minute before this place is littered with federal agents, and local law enforcement."

Chief Humphries appeared at the side door to shut it, and said, "I am staying behind. I am all washed up anyway. I will buy you at least a few minutes, now GO!"

Turning to Commander Teale, Chief Humphries said, "Commander, if you live through all of this, please clear my name. All I have left if my dignity. That is all I ask. Now get the hell out of here!"

Chief Humphries closed the side door, and banged the van with the side of his fist, as Augustus tore away from the hospital.

Kneeling to pick up the dead NSA agent's M-4 carbine rifle, Chief Humphries coughed violently, and spit blood onto the ground.

"Hurry up you bastards," Chief Humphries said, wiping his mouth. "I don't have long to go."

⌘⌘⌘

TWENTY-TWO

The thunderous sound of footsteps grew louder by the nanosecond as federal agents approached the hospital loading dock area.

The first set of agents to come into view lowered their weapons upon seeing the shiny, golden federal law enforcement badge hanging over Chief Humphries' chest.

Chief Humphries stood over the dead NSA agent, saying, "I am Chief Warrant Officer Patrick Humphries with Coast Guard Investigative Service. This man was a murderous traitor, and he is now dead."

Unclear as to what he may have stumbled upon, an agent slowly raised his weapon as he crept towards Chief Humphries.

"Chief Humphries," the agent said. "Please back away from the body."

Chief Humphries raised his weapon, and aimed it at the agent while saying, "Negative, young man. This is an extremely sensitive situation, and there are a lot of unclean hands involved in this fiasco. I need to meet with DSAC Wilkerson. Only he can hear what I know about this individual."

He then trained his weapon in the direction from which additional footsteps could be heard approaching the area.

"Chief Humphries, what is the meaning of all this?" COG Mason shouted.

"Mason," Chief Humphries replied. "I need DSAC Wilkerson to come here right now. I have acquired actionable intelligence for his ears only."

Chief Humphries retrieved a digital recorder from his pocket, saying, "I took this off our dead NSA friend here. Only DSAC Wilkerson is cleared to hear what it contains."

COG Mason nodded, and said, "Everyone, stand down. I am going to get DSAC Wilkerson here on the double."

To Chief Humphries, COG Mason asked, "The protectee, where is he?"

"I had Commander Teale take him to the home of Augustus Peña's mother for the time being, since there is already a protective detail stationed there for her security," replied Chief Humphries.

"Makes sense," COG Mason replied. He then placed a call to DSAC Wilkerson.

❧❧❧

A black, oversized government SUV flashed its emergency lights as it raced through the Des Moines city streets towards the hospital.

Inside, seated at the rear, was DSAC Wilkerson. He was eager to learn of the actionable intelligence that Chief Humphries claimed to have obtained.

He was also giving thought to what COG Mason told him regarding the commander taking Chad Molander to Noemi Peña's home for protection.

"Well, we were going to get them anyway," DSAC Wilkerson delightedly said. "Three birds with one stone. This is turning out to be a very good night."

DSAC Wilkerson retrieved a phone from his pocket, and placed a call. He then said to the person on the other end of the line, "Send a team to the mother's home. There are three targets there. Maybe your guys can do something right tonight, and make their kills, instead of getting themselves whacked like what happened at Commander Teale's home earlier tonight."

❧❧❧

DSAC Wilkerson exited the vehicle, and said, "What do you have there, Chief Humphries?"

"A dead traitor," Chief Humphries replied, coughing heavily.

"You don't look too good," DSAC Wilkerson said.

"I'm not, but thank you for noticing," Chief Humphries replied, coughing more blood onto the ground.

"For Christ's sake, go inside and get help!" DSAC Wilkerson demanded.

"There is no help for me, David. I am at the end," said Chief Humphries, referring to the DSAC by his first name.

DSAC Wilkerson also referred to the Chief by his first name. "Patrick, look, I need for you to –."

"No, David, stop right there," Chief Humphries demanded. "You need to hear this. Only you possess the required security clearance to hear this."

Chief Humphries tossed the digital recorder at him.

DSAC Wilkerson caught it, looked it over, and raised it to his ears as he hit the play button.

The recording played for two minutes. DSAC Wilkerson's eyes revealed anger, and fear.

The digital recorder contained a compilation of telephone conversations between DSAC Wilkerson, and various individuals. The subject matter of the conversations ranged from the affair DSAC Wilkerson had with Chief Humphries' ex-wife, to all things related to the Augustus Peña matter.

"How did you –?" DSAC Wilkerson started to ask.

"You are not the only one who can play dirty, David," Chief Humphries replied. "I knew from the inception that you were banging my now ex-wife. But I also knew something else, David. That you could never be anything other that a corrupt cop. Consequently, I had Augustus call in a few favors…to pull a large sampling of your depravity for the world to hear. And there it is, David. You are in deep on the attempt to assassinate Augustus Peña, and are equally as guilty for all the other deaths that have occurred as a result."

Chief Humphries coughed harder than he ever had, and fell onto the corpse by his feet. He quickly steadied himself, and trained his weapon on DSAC Wilkerson.

"Oh, and by the way," Chief Humphries said. "One final thing. We also know that your boys are headed to Mrs. Peña's house as we speak."

DSAC Wilkerson dropped the digital recorder, reached for his handgun, and yelled, "You piece of shit, sonofabitch!"

But he barely got it out of its holster before Chief Humphries shot several rounds into the DSAC's chest, neck, and face…killing him instantly.

The surrounding agents raised their weapons, preparing to fire.

COG Mason pleaded with Chief Humphries to not escalate the matter further.

But Chief Humphries already planned for how this was going to end. He aimed his weapon towards the agents, knowing full well they had no choice other than to shoot him.

Spitting out blood, CGIS Chief Warrant Officer Patrick Humphries said, "Don't miss, you bunch of pathetic sheep."

⁊⁊⁊⁊

The FPS agents guarding the perimeter of Noemi Peña's home looked skyward upon hearing the MH-6 Littlebird special operations helicopter approach.

"That was fast," said FPS Agent Morelli.

The small helicopter barely touched down on the lawn, and three tactical operators jumped off. The MH-6 Littlebird then sped back up into the sky, as the men ran towards the house.

"I need three of your men to enter with us, to stop anyone from leaving house as we clear through it," demanded the lead tactical operator. "We have intelligence that suggests an enemy has breached your perimeter, and entered the home."

"I'm on it," replied FPS Agent Morelli. He then summoned two FPS agents to accompany him, and the three tactical operators, into the house.

⁊⁊⁊⁊

One by one the FPS agents, and tactical operators, entered Noemi Peña's home.

Once inside, the lead tactical operator said to FPS Agent Morelli, "Cover this door, and the windows on the other side of this room. We are going in to see if the three protected individuals are still alive."

"Sir," said FPS Agent Morelli to the lead tactical operator. "The only occupant in this home is the protectee. She has no one else in here with her. The only other person to visit tonight was a Chief Warrant Officer with CGIS, at the direction of DSAC Wilkerson. But he has been gone now for several hours."

"Are you saying that a wheelchair-bound protectee was not delivered here tonight for you to guard?" The lead tactical operator asked.

"Definitely not," replied FPS Agent Morelli.

In the kitchen, an appliance beeped.

In the basement, a loud, mechanical hissing sound boomed throughout the house, causing the wood paneling to moan.

The lead tactical operator looked at his men, and said, "No fucking way."

⌘⌘⌘

TWENTY-THREE

An alarm sound emanated from Noemi Peña's mobile phone.

"The security app on your phone is going off, ma," Augustus said to her, as he exited the freeway.

Noemi Peña looked at her phone's notification. It alerted her to an unauthorized entry into her house. Having already been briefed on its significance by her son, she sighed, and said, "I am really glad that I brought my Winchester. It is the only thing I am going to have left, carajo."

"Do it now, ma!" Augustus demanded.

"Adios, pendejos," Noemi said, as she depressed the GO button on a separate application that Augustus had downloaded onto her smartphone, which served as a detonator.

ૡ૰ૡ૰ૡ૰

Augustus drove the van onto a private airstrip located in the Des Moines suburb of Ankeny.

On the tarmac, a Dassault Falcon2000S model jet was fueled, and ready to go.

The jetliner's doorway opened, and a staircase lowered for the passengers to board.

Upon settling Noemi, and Chad, into their seats, Augustus turned to Commander Teale to shake his hand, and thank him.

"Do not even think about saying it," said Commander Teale. "You and I have lost way too much. It is time that we return the favor. I will stay the course, 'Director' Peña, as I know you will. You can trust me when I say that I will."

"I believe you, commander," replied Augustus. "Maybe, someday, you and I can sit down and share a long, hard cry over all of this."

Commander Teale nodded in agreement, and exited the airplane.

ૡ૰ૡ૰ૡ૰

Augustus latched the jet door shut, and went into the cockpit.

"We are ready when you are," Augustus said to Jonah Spraggs, who was piloting the aircraft.

"Roger that," replied Jonah. "Did the intel I extracted from the prisoner provide you with what you need?"

"It provided me with enough to go on," replied Augustus. "When we land, I will transfer my mother, and Chad Molander, to the protective custody of a man named Haaris. I can vouch for him, Jonah, so be cool, okay?"

"I will, mister Peña," Jonah sheepishly replied.

Augustus then said, "Once they are all on their way, I need you to take me to another airstrip."

"No problem at all," said Jonah. "I haven't flown this much since my missions in Colombia, and Nicaragua several years ago. I'm pumped. Besides, my connections at NTSB have removed this plane from the proverbial grid for four days. No one will be able to track us."

Augustus said, "You and I are going to make an excellent team. Which reminds me. The prisoner, Jericho. Has he been dealt with?"

"He is as dead as a doornail, Mr. Peña, and spread out like fertilizer across the prairie," Jonah replied. "Where are we headed after we drop them off?"

"Sugarland, Texas," Augustus replied.

ۻۻۻ

Jonah Spraggs flawlessly executed the private jet's takeoff from the limited sized runway.

Once they were fully airborne, Augustus asked, "Does this classy jet come with satellite radio?"

"Hell yes," replied Jonah, showing Augustus where on the control panel to find the dials.

Augustus searched the available channels, and came upon a central Iowa news broadcast.

> "Authorities are now confirming that the explosion which levelled a Des Moines home, causing damage to several others in the area, was in

fact the residence of Noemi Peña, the mother of former Iowa Safety and Intelligence Bureau Director Augustus Peña. Officials have refused to comment on whether this destruction is tied in any way to the recent tragedies that have befallen the Peña family."

"One local expert, who has no actual knowledge of what occurred at the Peña residence, spoke to us here at KBTI to offer his opinion:"

"It is very possible that the explosion occurred due to human error, since it is well known that several pipefitting contractors have been working in the area, installing new piping to support the relocation of gas meters from nearby residences, and businesses. All it really takes is for a pressurized full-flow gas pipe to be opened, with no method for mitigating the release of gas, to cause a destructive blast such as this."

"It is currently unknown whether the home of Noemi Peña was occupied at the time of the blast, or of any possible injuries associated with it. This is a developing story, and we will provide you with updated information as it becomes available to our newsroom."

"Turning to national news. The U.S. Army says that pilot fatigue, combined with treacherous weather conditions, are to blame for the downing of two special forces Blackhawk helicopters that were on routine training maneuvers in North Dakota earlier this month. The U.S. Army states that, in light of these tragic training accidents, a commission will be put together to evaluate when, and how, pilots train, as well as to monitor the competency levels of pilots who are tasked to train in such treacherous weather conditions."

Augustus turned off the radio, and said, "No mention of the hospital incident, or of Commander Teale's wife. Typical."

Jonah shook his head, saying, "The stuff they did talk about, though. Man, I will never listen to the news the same way again. That's for sure."

Augustus chuckled as a memory came back to him. He then said, "My wife told me the same thing, Jonah, years ago when I taught her how to listen to the news if she wanted to know where I was."

Jonah looked back towards the passenger compartment, where he observed Chad Molander sleeping, and Noemi Peña looking around, with the Winchester rifle laid across her lap.

"You should probably get that, and put it away, so that it doesn't go off accidentally, and bring down the plane," Jonah said, referring to the rifle.

"Good luck getting that fucking thing from her, brother!" Augustus said, bellowing with laughter.

Like a ghost dancing about the clouds, the jet zoomed towards its destination; to a place where no harm would ever come to Noemi Peña, or Chad Molander.

⌘⌘⌘

TWENTY-FOUR

Micah Ward had been appointed by the Iowa Governor to the position of Interim Director for the Iowa Safety and Intelligence Bureau (Bureau). His task was to temporarily lead the Bureau until a full political appointment to replace Augustus Peña was decided upon.

"What a freaking mess," Interim Director Ward said, tossing a local newspaper onto his desk.

Plastered on practically every page of the newspaper were photos of various crime scenes associated with the Augustus Peña matter.

"I don't know which is worse, the photographs, or the headlines," he said, looking out his window at the golden dome of the Iowa Capitol building.

One headline read: "Family of Iowa State Patrol commander slaughtered by cartel assassins seeking to locate Augustus Peña. The whereabouts of the commander are unknown."

An equally intriguing headline read: "Augustus Peña's wife, and child, murdered prior to the former director's mother dying in an explosion."

To Interim Director Ward, the circus of articles seemed more appropriate for a tabloid publication, than a highly respected newspaper like the one on his desk.

"The feds have yet to officially request assistance from the Bureau," Interim Director Ward said, "but it is just a matter of time. This whole thing is way too convoluted to not require assistance from local intelligence authorities."

Interim Director Ward's computer dinged with a notification from the Bureau's internal messaging platform. He went to his computer, and read the message. It was from the security desk located in the lobby.

LOBBY: "Sir, you have two visitors."

INTERIM DIRECTOR WARD: "Who?"

LOBBY: "Feds. Intelligence. No names given. Only pictures on their credentials. They say there is an urgent, and top-secret matter to discuss with you. Also, one of them has his head bandaged from an injury, so I cannot confirm facial identity with the photo on his credential."

INTERIM DIRECTOR WARD: "Interesting…"

LOBBY: "Protocol dictates that I turn them away, and obtain contact information for them. Is this how you wish for me to proceed?"

Interim Director Ward considered his options while looking at the blinking cursor, and then typed:

INTERIM DIRECTOR WARD: "Negative. I will be down in fifteen minutes. Get them settled into the soundproof conference room behind you. Also, please have two troopers stationed in the room as well."

LOBBY: "Roger. Will do."

Interim Director Ward sat down to ponder the reason for this unscheduled visit from the feds.
"Undoubtedly, it has something to do with this whole thing," he surmised, picking up the newspaper from his desk.
Tossing it back onto his desk, he said, "I really don't think I need troopers stationed in the conference room. However, with so many officials being targeted for assassination recently, to include the man who previously occupied this seat, I cannot be too cautious."
He then checked the handgun in his holster, put on his suit jacket, and went downstairs to greet his visitors.

≈≈≈

Interim Director Ward entered the conference room, made his way to the long, rectangular table, and sat down.

Seated across from him were his two visitors. They spoke quietly to each other.

Interim Director Ward acknowledged the two state troopers by nodding at them. He then spoke. "I understand you have an urgent, top-secret matter to discuss with me."

The man without the bandaged head said, "Interim Director Ward, my name is Mason Weathers. I was assigned as the ground commander at the hospital where your Bureau's former deputy director was recently treated."

"COG Mason, yes! I heard about you," replied Interim Director Ward. "However, since the Bureau was not involved with the protective mission, you and I did not have the opportunity to meet. Welcome. How can I help you?"

Looking at his bandaged companion, COG Mason said, "Security is lacking all around us. I mean no disrespect to these proud troopers, but can we be alone?"

Interim Director Ward's demeanor changed. He became defensive, saying, "I am sorry, but that is not possible. As you said, security is lacking all around us. Have you seen the news lately? Besides, we have protocols in place here. I have already sidestepped protocol by granting both of you a visit with me without properly identifying yourselves."

"The news?" COG Mason retorted. "Never mind seeing it, Interim Director Ward. I am living it. Are you not aware of all that happened at the hospital with former Deputy Director Molander? The news...I am about to generate more of it. Now please, can you, this man, and I have absolute privacy?"

Confused, Interim Director Ward asked, "You are about to generate more of it? What does that even mean?"

COG Mason stepped around the table, and whispered into his ear.

Interim Director Ward stumbled backwards, and looked at his visitors with childlike enthusiasm. He then ordered the two troopers to exit the conference room, and to stand watch in the hallway.

❧❧❧

"I assume there are cameras in this room," COG Mason said.

"There are," confirmed Interim Director Ward. "However, they need to be manually activated from here," he said, revealing a console with various dials.

"Good," replied COG Mason. "Keep them off. You and I are to be the only people privy to this."

COG Mason removed the head bandages from the man that accompanied him.

"I thought I was going to suffocate under those things," Commander Teale protested. "You had those on me pretty snug."

"I needed to be certain they didn't slip off to reveal your identity," replied COG Mason.

He then said, "Interim Director Ward, I know you have limited authority when it comes to committing resources. However, there is something happening here that requires immediate attention at your level. Quite frankly, we do not have time to wait for the governor to make a full political appointment into your chair."

"Commander Teale," said COG Mason. "Would you please brief the interim director."

Commander Teale then said, "Interim Director Ward, you are going to want to sit down for this."

❧❧❧

Commander Teale briefed Interim Director Ward on everything he learned regarding the Augustus Peña matter.

He explained the reasoning for the original attacks against the Peña family.

He described what he understood about The Station, and all that occurred there.

He explained why Augustus killed two NSA assassins, who presented themselves to Commander Teale as agents with the U.S. Department of Homeland Security.

Finally, Commander Teale got to the subject of the winning jackpot lottery ticket, and its significance to the case.

"And that is where we are at right now, Interim Director Ward," said Commander Teale in a tired sounding voice.

"My wife," he continued, "was murdered because I probed too deep. I touched some nerves high up in the federal government. Consequently, they…whoever *THEY* are, wanted me dead. What they got instead was my wife. My innocent, darling wife. I've seen the news reports. It had absolutely nothing to do with drug cartels. But it had everything to do with a campaign of targeted execution, driven by people in charge of our nation's security, and I am here to expose it. It is not known beyond these walls whether I am dead or alive. All that is known is that I am missing. Interim Director Ward, I need for it to remain that way for at least a little while longer. I am waiting on some developments so that I can see this thing through."

"What exactly are you waiting on?" Interim Director Ward asked.

"I am waiting on you to make a decisive move."

"So am I," said COG Mason.

"I don't quite understand," said Interim Director Ward.

"The waters are muddied," said Commander Teale. "We have a good idea who is involved, but only at the surface level. We need to go deeper. We are just scratching the surface. The intelligence we have points us to the periphery of a much larger crises. A level of institutional corruption, and depravity that is almost inconceivable. Yet, it exists, and it is playing out right here in Iowa, in our backyard."

Commander Teale leaned in, saying, "And I mean literally, in our backyard, mister interim director."

Interim Director Ward shook his head, indicating he needed clarification.

Commander Teale explained further. "The Iowa Lottery Agency is literally behind this building. At some point, someone will come to claim the jackpot. That is a lot of money, and people have already died for it. And, as you may know, Iowa law requires that anyone claiming a jackpot prize must make the claim within one year from the lottery drawing, and reveal their identity. It is at that point, if someone does in fact show up to make a claim, that the real investigation begins, seeing as how we know that the original purchaser is dead, and that the ticket subsequently passed through the hands of assassins."

Interim Director Ward sprung to his feet, and picked up his office phone to connect with his secretary, saying, "I need to get in touch with the Iowa Lottery Commissioner, immediately!"

⌘⌘⌘

TWENTY-FIVE

It was one o'clock in the afternoon on a bright, sunshine filled day in Sugar Land, Texas.

Maureen Robertson, Senior Tax Partner with the multinational professional services firm Reed & Wattles, hustled across the firm's parking lot to get to her car. Meetings cluttered her daily calendar, reflecting her recent promotion to this position. But today was busier than usual.

On this day, Maureen had already met with a client, after speaking at an early breakfast conference. Maureen's afternoon, however, was scheduled to be consumed consulting her most important client.

Fumbling through her purse for her oversized sunglasses to shield her sensitive blue eyes from the sun, she cursed, "Shit, I am so late to this meeting. Of all the times for me to be late to a client meeting, this one ain't it."

Maureen got into her new luxury sports car, and revved the engine. Fixated with the vehicle's power and speed, Maureen smiled, and spoke to it.

"There now, hon. You just make everything feel right again. You be sure to get momma to her meeting as quickly as you can. Afterwards, we can go on a nice, real fast drive."

Maureen placed the vehicle in reverse, but quickly shifted back into park upon receiving a phone text from her client.

CLIENT: "You are late."

"Aw, no," Maureen said. "These XM folks are not the kind you leave waiting around. Good Lord."

Nervously, she began to text a response when another text from her client came through.

CLIENT: "Time is of the essence. We must change the location of our meeting."

Maureen typed a response.

MAUREEN: "Okay. Where?"

CLIENT: "Right here, in your car."

ৡৡৡ

Augustus drove Maureen's luxury sports car to a warehouse he rented under a fictitious identity.

In the back seat, Maureen snored heavily from the sedative Augustus injected into her neck.

Augustus pulled the luxury sports car into the warehouse, and closed its white, metallic garage door.

Towards the rear of the warehouse was a small, windowless office complete with a desk, and two chairs.

Augustus checked to make sure they were alone. Satisfied that they were, he pulled Maureen from the car, and carried her to the office.

He then propped Maureen into a chair, and injected her in the neck with a solution to wake her up.

ৡৡৡ

Maureen arose from her drug-induced stupor. The room spun wildly, and her eyes swirled under her eyelids. She gagged, and spit up bile onto her expensive skirt suit.

"Hi Maureen," Augustus said. "You shouldn't be late to your meetings. It is rude, and this is what happens when we have to make up for lost time."

Augustus forced water into her mouth, saying, "Here you go. Drink this. It will make you feel better."

"What are you going to do with me, you sick pervert?" Maureen shouted.

Augustus replied, "Me? Oh, not much else, I hope. I am a gentle soul, Maureen. I simply needed to obtain your undivided attention. But the people you provide services for, XM Investments, well…they are a different story altogether. I cannot vouch for what they will, or will not, do to a pretty little thing like you once they learn of our intimate meeting today."

"What in the world? Are you insane?" Maureen cried.

"A little bit, yes, Maureen. Thank you for noticing. You see, I have always been a little loco en la cabeza. However, after your client, XM...you do know who I am talking about, do you not, Maureen? The group out of Belize?"

"Yes!" Maureen shouted.

"Muy chevere, very good," Augustus replied. "Well, they, XM, tried to kill me, and my family...and that kind of shit makes a person a little fucking insane!"

Augustus' nose touched Maureen's as he shouted these words, causing her to weep uncontrollably.

Augustus continued speaking. "XM is not an investment consortium, as their name suggests. But you probably already know that. No. XM Investments is a syndicate of assassins. Killers, hired by governments around the world, including ours, that are too feeble to do their own dirty work."

"What do you do for them, Maureen?" Augustus asked.

"I assist them with financial matters," she cried.

"Do you also kill for them, Maureen?" Augustus tauntingly asked, knowing the answer.

Maureen replied, "God, no! I had no idea what they did. All they ever asked of me was to, you know, hide money, and move it around within various accounts. I really do not know who they are. I mean, I have only met someone in person once. But that was a few years ago. Today was going to be the second time I physically met with someone from XM Investments. But I guess that wasn't a real meeting after all."

"What else?" Augustus demanded.

Maureen cried, "That's all, I swear to you mister. That is all I ever did for them, and this is all I know."

"You must have a contact at XM to report any financial irregularities," Augustus pressed.

Maureen shifted, and begged, "Please, no. I can't."

"Then I guess I have no choice but to get kind of rough on you, and make it look as if you were murdered by a group of horny thugs from the hood, Maureen." Augustus threatened. "There will be no questions asked. Little white woman like you in this neighborhood. Shit like that happens all the time, and nobody blinks an eye."

"RODRIGO!" Maureen screamed. "The contact I report to at XM, he goes by Rodrigo. I have no idea if that is his real name, or if this is his first, or last name. But that is who I contact, and no one else."

"You told me earlier that you only met an XM representative in person once. Was it him?" Augustus asked.

"Yes," Maureen answered.

"How do you make contact with him?" Augustus asked.

Maureen answered, "I have to say his name five times in a row into my smartphone. I then type into my number pad a four-digit code he gave me. An application then appears on my phone screen, and I type what I need to report into a limited-space text field within it."

"Slick," Augustus said. "Get yourself gathered together because you about to make a financial report to your boy Rodrigo."

⌘⌘⌘

TWENTY-SIX

Rodrigo meticulously puffed on a cigar as he waited to board a private jet to the Cayman Islands. The scent of his favorite Dominican cigar caused him to smile as smoke from it wafted across his face.

Feeling a buzz on his hip from the ridiculously large phone clipped to his pants, Rodrigo unceremoniously exhaled, and answered the call.

"Si," Rodrigo said.

"A most interesting message has just been transmitted to you via our application. It is from our financial arranger in the United States," said Áhari.

"Is it related to the most recent events there involving our personnel?" Rodrigo asked.

"It most certainly is," Áhari replied. "It appears that not all personnel were lost, as we had been previously advised."

"I will review the message through my server," said Rodrigo. "I will speak with you afterwards."

"As you wish," replied Áhari.

ॐ ॐ ॐ

Once airborne, Rodrigo accessed the application to review the message from Maureen. The message read:

"I have in my possession a winning jackpot lottery ticket from the State of Iowa. It was handed to me by a man named Jericho. He wished for me to tell you that his entire team died obtaining this ticket for you. He also wished for me to tell you to go to Hell, and that he quit. The lottery drawing was in December of last year. I have checked the lottery website, and can confirm it is a winner worth 16.5 million U.S. dollars. Request instructions on how to proceed."

Rodrigo called Áhari to discuss the message. After the two men agreed upon a course of action, Rodrigo transmitted his response to Maureen.

> "My associate, Áhari, will meet you to collect the ticket. Please go to the marina in Galveston, TX in four days, during the noon hour. He will be on the boat where you and I met."

☙☙☙

At the warehouse, Maureen read Rodrigo's response aloud.

Augustus smiled, and told her, "Now, I need for you to make a call to this number, and read from the script I prepared for you, word for word."

☙☙☙

C. Virgil Milken breathed hard as he ran across the long corridor leading to NICO headquarters, codenamed The Chamber.

Checking his watch at the end of corridor, at the sentry checkpoint, Milken impatiently growled, "Come on, come on, come on."

At the checkpoint, a sentinel dutifully scanned Milken's palm to verify his identity while saying, "These protocols are necessary, even for you, Mr. Milken. So, please, remain calm, and allow us to perform our duty."

Milken nodded in acknowledgement. He then looked up to the sniper that, also per protocol, had him in his sights should Milken fail to be cleared for entry into The Chamber.

Milken remembered how months prior he had been perched in that very same sniper's nest awaiting the arrival of Maxwell Prater, NICO's former Chief of Asset Control, before assassinating him. He then said, "Karma would be unreasonably cruel if this is how I go out, after coming so close to ending the Augustus Peña matter."

"You are clear, sir," said the sentinel. "You are free to pass."

☙☙☙

"Ah, well, here comes the Master of Ceremonies himself," mused Prentiss Gates.

"Cut the shit," replied Milken. "We have some very serious business to address."

Saxby Coles, NICO's Ambassador of External Affairs, called the meeting to order.

Seated around the table were the remaining NICO leaders who voted to sanction the assassination of Augustus Peña, at Milken's behest.

"We all know why we are here," Milken said, looking each of them in the eye. "The Augustus Peña operation has not aged well. We picked a fight, and got our asses kicked, plain and simple. There is no more to it than that."

Milken sat down, saying, "Prentiss, Saxby, the rest of you…it is time to end this. The information I am receiving from our birddogs in Iowa is that we are quickly losing our edge at containing this from the public. We are one degree of separation from having everything exposed if we do not shut this down fast."

"You should have just let Augustus write his novels. It sounds as if we are more effective at revealing ourselves to the world than what Augustus could have accomplished with some quasi-fictional books," Prentiss said.

Before Milken could pounce on Prentiss, Saxby Coles said, "I concur with his assessment, Milken. If we could have –."

"Enough!" Milken shouted. "It is too late to bicker about this. We did it. We failed. It is time to end it."

"What do you have up your sleeve this time, Virg?" Prentiss asked.

Milken answered, "I received word from XM that they are ceasing all U.S. operations, effective immediately. All methods of electronic communications used to contact them have been destroyed, to include their dedicated spy satellites for our region. XM techs are frying those satellites in orbit as we speak."

"How does that help us right now?" I don't get it," said Saxby.

Milken replied, "XM has compiled a list of thirty individuals, whom are not a part of our apparatus, but who have gleaned enough information to make our existence known. XM also has location information for these individuals. The last element of XM leadership within the United States is leaving in four days. He will have that information for us if we want it. I intend on going to get it."

Incredulous, Prentiss asked, "And do what with it, Virg? For Christ's sake, didn't you just say you wanted to stop all of this, and move on? You are allowing our failure to kill Augusts to unravel you!"

Milken slammed the table, yelling, "No! That is not what I said. I told you that I want to end this, and that is what I am going to do. I will obtain the list. I will locate, and monitor the individuals in question. And I will kill them until no one who believes they have stumbled upon a great government conspiracy to commit targeted assassinations remains alive!"

"Now," Milken ordered as he cocked the hammer on his sidearm. "All in favor, say aye,"

In unison, the NICO leadership answered, "Aye."

⌘⌘⌘

TWENTY-SEVEN

Maureen Robertson sobbed after sending her messages to XM, and NICO.

"Do you feel bad for what you just did?" Augustus asked.

"To the contrary," Maureen replied. "After learning from you their true business, I feel an overwhelming sense of good. But I also feel very afraid."

"You should feel good," said Augustus. "And you are wise to feel afraid. They are going to kill you. In fact, in my professional opinion, they would have killed you at some point in the future anyway…even if I had not entered your life. You have gained too much knowledge about their financial practices over time. That is not a risk that XM would be willing to take."

"Is there anything I can do?" Maureen pleaded.

"Your best chance is to help me blow this wide open," Augustus replied.

"I only handle tax shelters, and movement of money. Most of the transactions are obfuscated. Masked with limited traceability. None of the information I have can help you blow anything wide open, mister," Maureen said.

"This lottery ticket," Augustus said, holding it for her to see. "Go cash it. Claim it on behalf of your client, XM Investments."

"Why in the world would I –," asked Maureen before Augustus interrupted.

"The less you know, the better," Augustus said.

"It doesn't matter anyhow, because that is not how I would handle any sort of claims for any of my clients," Maureen protested.

"What do you mean?" Augustus asked.

"Like I said, mister. I handle tax, and money movement once liquid assets are transferred to me. Something like this here jackpot lottery ticket would be a legal claim to receive monetary assets owed to the client. And that is not for me to do," explained Maureen.

"Then who does handle it?" Augustus pressed.

"XM has an attorney on retainer. He is rarely needed. But he is an international legal powerhouse, and is ready to work at a moment's notice," Maureen replied.

"Is the lawyer nearby?" Augustus asked.

"No," Maureen answered. "He lives in Savannah, Georgia. But he has a fictitious law practice registered in upstate New York. I will need to send that ticket to him via armed courier, with specific instructions on how to proceed."

Augustus looked at the jackpot lottery ticket in his hand. He then kissed the ticket, and speaking to it said, "You are my only hope." He then handed the ticket to Maureen.

"In case you are worried about my trying to cash this in for myself...don't," Maureen said. "I know full well that I would barely be able to spend one dollar of it before I ended up in a river somewhere."

"More like end up in the shit pile of a lion's den," Augustus mused. "But I'm glad that you understand."

Augustus handed Maureen her car keys, saying, "It has been a pleasure, Ms. Maureen Robertson."

She responded, "Likewise, Mr. Augustus Peña."

⌘⌘⌘

TWENTY-EIGHT

Áhari docked his yacht, named La Gros Pittón, at the Galveston, Texas marina.

He was to meet Maureen Robertson the next day to retrieve the jackpot lottery ticket from her. He did not want to be late for that meeting.

Moreover, Áhari needed to acquaint himself with the marina's layout. He planned on killing Maureen with drugs, and dumping her body to make it appear as if she died of an overdose. He needed to find a good spot to place her.

Once ashore, Áhari casually strolled along the boardwalk, tipping his ivory fedora hat to the throngs of pretty women that passed him by.

After identifying several ideal locations along the docks fitting for an overdose victim, Áhari sat on a bench to think through the details of getting this done.

Satisfied that he had a solid plan in place, Áhari returned to his yacht.

అఛఛఛ

Áhari was hungry, and intended on preparing a meal in the galley of his vessel. However, as he approached his yacht, he quickly lost his appetite upon noticing movement from within.

Áhari stopped walking, removed his hat, and retrieved a .22 Magnum Derringer he kept tucked in the lining.

Placing his hat back on, Áhari checked his weapon, and crept forward on the creaky marina boardwalk.

Suddenly, an older looking man stepped out onto the Yacht's deck, saying, "My, my, my…La Gros Pittón. What does that mean, anyway? The large bird? It sounds French. Is it French? Also, is this papaya? This stuff is good."

Áhari was stunned. He had no idea who this crazy American was, or why he was on his yacht, eating his fruit.

The man continued to speak: "You boys know how to do it right. Amen to that, let me tell you. I am hoping for something like this upon my retirement. But that cannot happen until I get through that list you have for me."

Áhari returned his gun to the inner lining of his hat, and boarded his yacht, saying, "If you are looking for a party boat, this one is not it. Please remove yourself from my yacht. I will not harm you if you quickly comply."

"Harm me? Quickly comply? Why…who do you think you are talking to?"

"Please," Áhari insisted. "Do it now."

"Now hold on! You invited me here so that I can get intelligence from you. But now you are threatening me? Is everyone out of Belize bat shit crazy?"

"Who are you, please?" Áhari asked.

"My name is Milken. I know for damn sure you are not Rodrigo. So, the question really becomes this: Who the fuck are you?"

Milken did not wait for a response, and continued speaking. "You don't have a list of names for me, do you?"

"I most certainly do not," replied Áhari.

Milken then asked, "And I suppose that neither you, nor anyone else from XM Investments, communicated with me via my private satellite server to provide me with the name of this vessel, and to inform me that you would be here a day early?"

Neither man said a word until Milken screamed, "Augustus!"

ॐॐॐ

The explosion rocked the marina, engulfing several nearby yachts in an inferno.

Augustus treaded water for several minutes after the blast to make sure there were no survivors.

Seeing nothing but destruction, Augustus placed the oxygen snorkel from his scuba gear into his mouth.

Descending into the depths of the Gulf of Mexico, Augustus silently swam to his next destination.

⌘⌘⌘

TWENTY-NINE

Seated in his den's plush leather recliner, enjoying a snifter of brandy, was attorney Clayton Hicks. Looking out his window, he was fixated on the possible motives of the man walking up his long, curved driveway.

"He does not appear to be your typical delivery person," Clayton said aloud, sipping his brandy. "The lay delivery person does not carry a gun on their hip like this here fellow."

The man got closer to his house. Clayton rose from his chair to view the man from a better angle.

Looking down at the man as he rang the doorbell, Clayton said, "He could very well be a home invader, albeit the worst ever."

Clayton then chugged the remainder of his brandy, and went to answer the door.

❧❧❧

Clayton tapped his chin with the envelope the courier just delivered. Looking at the man as he exited the property, Clayton sighed, and said:

"What a strange man. I wonder how much money a person like that can earn. I mean, truly. What is that man's earning potential? And the work he is doing. My word. Carrying a gun to deliver this envelope to me? Is he actually willing to shoot someone for receiving in return, what, the minimum wage perhaps?"

Clayton stumbled into his kitchen, and poured himself more brandy from a different bottle. He kept several throughout his lavish estate. All opened, and ready to pour.

Clayton sat down at the kitchen table with the envelope, and his freshly filled snifter of brandy. He then used his fat index finger to open the envelope, saying, "Where are you from, and what do you want from me?"

ൟൟൟ

Clayton dismissively flung the contents of the envelope across his kitchen, saying, "The absurdity, and offensive nature of this request is incomprehensible. How dare they disrespect me in such a manner as to expect me to travel to, where in the dickens was that?"

Clayton picked up the letter, and continued with his rant. "Iowa, to claim a lottery ticket?"

Clayton stomped to his living room, and tossed logs into his fireplace. He then poured himself another brandy from an open bottle on the mantle, and started a fire.

"The lottery. For good heavens. What sort of degenerate do they take me for? Only the dregs of society have the shameless audacity of purchasing a ticket in the hopes of winning grandness! But not me. I am an Ivy League scholar, an expert in international law, and diplomacy. It is in fact the very reason why XM chose me as their international legal guru. What, with my vast knowledge of Danish, Indian, and Caribbean laws, I was the obvious choice. A lottery ticket…what utter bollocks."

Clayton returned Maureen's letter, and the lottery ticket, into the envelope. He then brought the packaged envelope to the fireplace. He was about to toss it into the crackling fire when a thought occurred to him.

"Drat," he said, looking at the envelope. "They may want this back. Just because I will not undertake this menial task does not mean some peasant would not claim it for them. However, I will not dignify this shameless request of theirs with a response. My lack of action on this matter will require them to contact me, and at that time I will notify them of the offensive nature of this request. Perhaps they will send that fellow to pick it up. If they do, I will talk to that chap about the finer things in life, from having dignity in the work that you do to, well, excellent brandy of course!"

Clayton staggered upstairs to his den, and placed the envelope into a walled safe.

⌘⌘⌘

THIRTY

Augustus patiently waited in line at the U.S. Customs and Border Protection (CBP) Port of Entry in Naco, Arizona.

The late model pickup truck he drove reeked of whatever livestock the previous driver transported in it. To make matters worse, dark smoke plumed from its exhaust whilst the engine churned unhealthily, periodically emitting sounds indicating it was about to permanently break down.

A CBP Officer waved Augustus forward for inspection while holding a handkerchief to his face.

"Feel free to leave this piece of shit in Mexico next time, if you can understand what I am saying to you," the CBP Officer said.

"Entiendo," Augustus said in Spanish, indicating he understood.

Fifteen minutes later, the inspection was complete.

"Okay, Señor Vega. Todo se ve bien. Nosotros hemos terminado. Bienvenidos a los Estados Unidos," said a different CBP officer as he banged the truck, informing Augustus that everything looked good, and welcoming him to the United States.

"Muchas gracias," Augustus replied. He then drove through the Port of Entry, and onward into the town of Naco.

༄༄༄

Augustus was familiar with the town of Naco, Arizona, having visited it several times throughout his career.

He was also extremely fond of his destination on this day, the Saint Michael Mission.

The Mission was a place of solitude, and reflection for Augustus. Because of this, whenever he found himself in the vicinity, he would stop in to pray, and to reflect on what his life had become.

As he pulled the truck up to the Mission, he reflected on the last time he was there. It was right before he retired from NICO to pursue a political appointee position in Iowa.

"It feels like yesterday," said Augustus, as he placed the loud, smoky truck into park.

Augustus felt a deep connection to this place. Not only because of his previous visits, but because this is the last place where his lovely son Nathaniel was prior to being carted off to a life of safety. His son's energy was here, and Augustus wanted to feel it. He wanted to connect with Nathaniel's energy through prayer.

Moreover, his good friend died here, inside the Mission, after sacrificing so much for Augustus, and his family.

"The Bakers are an irreplaceable force for good in this world," Augustus said.

Looking up at the Mission's steeple, Augustus said, "This is a very appropriate location for such an honorable death, my friend. I pray that Saint Michael himself escorts your soul, and the souls of your sons Caleb and Bo, to Heaven. And that he asks God to appoint you all as generals in His army."

Augustus exited the truck, made the sign of the cross, and entered the Mission.

ﾊﾟﾊﾟﾊﾟ

Augustus sensed something wrong the moment he entered the Mission. Reacting quickly to a perceived threat, he dove forward on the hard floor.

But it was not fast enough, and his right leg was grazed by shotgun pellets.

The roar of the shotgun that fired those pellets caused a stained-glass window to crack.

The shooter reloaded, as evidenced by the racking sound of a shell being chambered, and of an expended casing hitting the floor.

Another blast from the shotgun nearly hit Augustus in the head. Shards of wood from pews shattered by the shotgun blast penetrated his skull, causing him to bleed.

Another re-load.

Another shot.

Finally, the shooter spoke as he dropped the shotgun to the floor.

"I have been shot twelve times, twice in the heart. I was held captive in a Gook prison camp run by the Russians during Nam. I have survived helicopter crashes, car wrecks, been blown up at least a dozen times. Hell...I even survived a big ole tornado that picked my ass up, and dropped me like a bad habit three counties away. And you know what, you little prick? Of all those near-death experiences, none pisses me off as much as that bullshit yacht explosion you pulled off in that shitty-ass marina."

Surprised, Augustus said, "Milken." His injuries causing him to slightly stammer his speech.

"You are goddamned right it is," replied Milken. "I am going to put buckshot right through your fucking spic head, Peña. But not before I have myself a little fun."

Augustus turned to stand and fight Milken, but his leg wound was much more severe than he had thought. Unable to stand, Augustus fell hard onto a pew alongside him.

Milken approached Augustus, while pulling a knife from his belt buckle. He then lunged at Augustus, and stabbed him three times in his left thigh.

Milken stood up, wiped sweat from his face, and said, "I knew you would come here after you thought I was dead. Once I learned that the oldest Baker died here, and not back at the compound as had been officially reported, there was no doubt in my mind that this place was part of your overall plan to save your family. It did not work out that well though, did it? Your wife may have been struck with a bout of luck by killing Ajax, my top assassin. But that bitches' luck ran out hard in that compound, didn't it?"

Augustus yelled, screamed, and cried all at once at the mention of his dead wife.

Milken continued. "Here, let me take your mind away from all that grief," he said, as he slammed Augustus' head against the floor, and cut off a piece of Augustus' left ear.

Augustus screamed even louder.

"This here is like old times, Augustus. It sure is," Milken said. "You know, people outside of our business always ask me if I served in Vietnam. I tell them, shit yes I did, and I fucking loved every minute of it."

෭෨෭෨෭෨

Augustus was helpless. He was gravely injured, and lost a lot of blood. He had no weapon, and was unable to fight back other than to periodically smack away Milken's knife thrusts.

"Well, enough fun has been had between us, amigo," Milken said. "It is time to bury this hatchet, and move on."

Milken walked to his shotgun, and picked it up. He then loaded a shell into its chamber, and said, "Oh, and by the way. I am going to hunt down your son, and carve him to pieces with this very knife. Isn't that lovely, Augustus? You and your son will have had pieces cut off you by the same knife."

Augustus knew that the end for him was near. He had killed many people as a NICO assassin, and knew when there was nothing more that could be done.

Augustus reeled from the thought of Milken murdering Nathaniel. But he did not want this to be his final thought. He refused to give the Devil the honor of sending him out of this world with such dread.

Instead, Augustus prayed to the Archangel Michael in Latin. "Sancte Michael Archangele, defende nos in proelio…"

"Seriously," Milken mockingly said. "You are going to pray. Alright, fine. I'll play along. Besides, the St. Michael prayer is one of my favorites. But I like my prayers in English."

Milken kicked Augustus over and, in English, repeated the verse Augustus had just prayed. "Saint Michael the Archangel, defend us in battle."

Augustus sat up, and continued with the prayer. "Contra nequitiam et insidias diaboli esto praesidium."

Milken interrupted, "Oh, this part is good," and then said, "Be our defense against the wickedness, and snares of the Devil."

Milken looked at Augustus, and said, "You're impressed, aren't you? I bet you didn't think I knew this mumbo jumbo shit, did you?" He then snorted, and said, "Go ahead, finish up. I ain't got all fucking day."

Augustus: "Imperet illi Deus supplices deprecamur."
Milken: "May God rebuke him, we humbly pray."
Augustus: "Tuque, Princeps militiae coelestis."
Milken: "And do thou, O Prince of the heavenly host."

Augustus: "Satanam aliosque spiritus malignos, qui ad perditionem animarum pervagantur in mundo, divina virtute in infernum detrude. Amen."

Milken: "This is some real good shit right here…By the power of God, cast into Hell Satan, and all evil spirits who prowl about the world seeking the ruin of souls. A-fucking-men."

Milken raised his shotgun. Aiming it at Augustus, he said, "I will see you in Hell, compadre. Be sure to tell the gang hello for me."

BOOM.

᪥᪥᪥

The devastating, and lethal shotgun blast stained the walls of the St. Michael Mission with blood.

The statues at the altar were not spared of ruin, as fragments of bone, teeth, and shotgun pellets removed large sections from them.

Augustus laid sprawled across the floor. His body, lifeless.

Suddenly, as if awakened from a nightmare, Augustus gasped for air. He then howled in pain from his wounds.

Grabbing onto his chest, Augustus tried to gain control of his breathing. He then touched his head to determine if the blood he saw on practically every surface around him was his.

It was not.

Augustus could barely move. He felt as if he were about to lose consciousness yet again. But he fought to stay awake.

Lying next to him, face down on the floor, with a massive hole through his back, was C. Virgil Milken. Smoke still fumed from his fresh wound.

Milken was dead.

Augustus strained, but managed to glance in the area behind where Milken last stood.

Standing in that place, with a shotgun in his hands, was a priest.

The priest knelt beside Milken to confirm his death. He then rose, and stepped alongside Augustus.

"You are an evil man," the priest said to him. "But God wishes to give you a chance at redemption."

The priest looked at Milken, and said, "That man was born of Satan, and was guided by him. I had no choice but to exact God's Will by taking his life."

"Who are you?" Augustus managed to ask before passing out.

The priest answered, "I am His Eminence Cardinal Marcus Lara, Archbishop of Sicily. I hold a seat at the ruling table of the Order that is protecting your son. You will be brought to a place where you will heal from your earthly wounds, which are great. But your greatest challenge, my son, will be to heal the wounds you have obtained upon your soul by defying God."

Cardinal Lara placed his weapon on the floor, and picked up Augustus.

Cradling Augustus like a child, Cardinal Lara said, "Come, my son. I will show you the Way."

⌘⌘⌘

THIRTY-ONE

DES MOINES, IOWA
SPRING, 2011

Iowa Lottery Commissioner Kevin Renalds slammed his office phone back onto its base. He then yelled for his executive officer to come into his office.

The executive officer appeared quickly, and asked, "Commissioner Renalds, what's wrong? Are you okay?"

Commissioner Renalds replied, "I need for you to get a hold of Special Agent Greg Jennings right now. Have him meet us over at the governor's mansion."

"Greg is in the field conducting a joint fraud investigation with the treasury department," replied the executive officer. "I am not certain I can connect with him right now."

"Well, you need to find a way," Commissioner Renalds snapped. "This is bigger than all of the fraud investigations our agency has ongoing combined."

Startled, the executive officer asked, "Can I ask what this is about?"

Commissioner Renalds replied, "You can ask, but I won't tell. Now, contact Greg so that we can get over to the governor's mansion. Move it!"

❧❧❧

Commissioner Renalds and his executive officer hustled across the capitol complex to the governor's mansion.

Upon their arrival, they were met by a black SUV, as it pulled up to the building's entrance. An Iowa state trooper exited the vehicle, and opened the rear passenger door.

Stanton Haynes, Iowa's longest-serving attorney general, exited the SUV. He then thanked the trooper, and spoke to Commissioner Renalds. "I tried my darndest to get Interim Director Ward from the Safety & Intelligence Bureau to tell me what the Devil all this drama is about, but he would not budge. However, seeing you here, I suspect that I might have an idea."

Commissioner Renalds nodded in a manner suggesting that he was on target.

Attorney General Haynes gestured toward the mansion's entrance, saying, "Well, then, let's get to it, shall we?"

෯෯෯

Upon entering the governor's mansion, the men were greeted in the foyer by Mildred Childs, Iowa's lieutenant governor.

"This has got to be huge if you are greeting us, as opposed to a staffer," opined Attorney General Haynes.

Lt. Governor Childs did not reply, other than to say, "Welcome, gentlemen. Please follow me. We will meet in the governor's den, which is located on the upper level."

As they walked, the front door flung open. Special Agent Greg Jennings breathed heavily, while saying, "Commissioner Renalds, I got here as fast as I could. I apologize for the delay."

Lt. Governor Childs eyeballed each of them, and stated, "I presume there will be no other staff coming from your respective agencies?"

Commissioner Renalds, and Attorney General Haynes answered in the affirmative, and the group made their way to the governor's den.

෯෯෯

The group arrived at the door of the governor's den. Waiting for them was Interim Director Ward.

He had a grim look on his face, and said, "The world you know, and the basic rules of decency amongst men you are accustomed to do not exist past these doors. I must warn you that your official positions do not matter once you enter. The only thing that matters is the composition of your moral character. Inasmuch as I would love to vouch for each of your moral convictions, I simply cannot. Consequently, you are all required to pass a polygraph test, to be administered by none other than me."

"Are you on drugs?" Attorney General Haynes protested.

"Honestly, I wish that I were," replied Interim Director Ward. "All of this would make so much more sense if that were the case."

Interim Director Ward then opened the doors before him, and led the group into the governor's den.

❧❧❧

Interim Director Ward administered the polygraph tests. Upon final confirmation that everyone passed, he and Lt. Governor Childs, led the group to an adjacent conference room.

Inside, a woman sat motionless towards the rear of the conference table.

Commissioner Renalds cleared his throat as everyone took their seats. He began to greet the woman, but Interim Director Ward interrupted him, saying:

"Gentlemen, this is Maureen Robertson. She is a Senior Tax Partner with a global services firm. Ms. Robertson provides top notch financial services for some extremely secretive, lucrative, and highly influential multi-national clients. She has some important information to share with us."

"Lord knows that I do love a good mystery now and then," said Attorney General Haynes. "But what I am itching to learn is why you have summoned the attorney general's office, as well as the lottery commission?"

Interim Director Ward turned to Maureen, and said, "I think this would be a good time to show them."

Maureen produced a smartphone from her purse. She then opened the phone's photo album application, selected a picture, and handed the phone to Attorney General Haynes.

Attorney General Haynes sprung to his feet. His eyes grew wide. He then handed the phone to Commissioner Renalds, and asked, "Is that Augustus Peña?"

"It sure as Hell is," replied Commissioner Renalds. "And he is posing with the jackpot winning Hot Ticket."

Commissioner Renalds then squinted while inspecting the photograph further, and asked, "What is that other paper Augustus is holding up? I can't read it."

Special Agent Jennings took the phone from Commissioner Renalds, inspected the photograph, and answered, "It says BELIEVE HER, PLEASE."

They all stared at Maureen Robertson, and huddled around her.

༄ ༄ ༄

For several hours Maureen explained, and detailed, the vast array of services she provided to XM Investments.

Maureen described with specificity her methods for contacting, and communicating with XM.

Finally, Maureen spoke of all that she knew regarding the jackpot lottery ticket, Augustus Peña's connection to it, and the canary traps that she, and Augustus, had put into play, to include the newsworthy explosion at the Galveston, Texas marina.

"This has all been very hard on you," said Interim Director Ward. "Unfortunately, it is going to get much more difficult. If what you have told us is true, then we are to expect a legal representative for XM Investments to come forward to claim the jackpot winnings on their behalf. I hope you understand that, until such time, we will need to place you in protective custody."

"Do you mean witness protection?" Maureen asked.

"No," replied Interim Director Ward. "That is a federal initiative. As you have demonstrated, the feds cannot be trusted. The fact of the matter is, Ms. Robertson, you need to remain in Iowa so that we can protect you."

"For how long?" Maureen asked.

Attorney General Haynes interjected, saying, "Iowa law requires that a winning lottery ticket be claimed within one year from the drawing date. So, to answer your question, until midnight on December 29th of this year."

Maureen pressed. "What happens if XM Investments smells a trap, and does not come forward to claim the jackpot by that time? Will I still receive protection?"

"No," answered Interim Director Ward. "You would not continue to receive protection. We can only protect you for the period during which a claim could be made. If no claim is made, we would have no option but to release you from protective custody."

Stunned, Maureen said, "So, if XM Investments happens to be dialed into Iowa law enforcement, and learns that I assisted you, they could feasibly wait until the expiration of the drawing anniversary to kill me? Is that what I am hearing?"

"I understand how this looks to you right now," said Attorney General Haynes. "But from what I have gathered from your statements here today, those folks would have already killed you had you not come to us."

Attorney General Haynes positioned his chair as close to Maureen as possible. He then leaned into her, and softly said:

"I certainly do not mean to be dismissive of your concerns. They are, in fact, very credible concerns. The danger you face is real. What is also real is that you escaped death by coming here. I am certain that this criminal syndicate from Belize is out there tying up loose ends after failing to physically acquire the jackpot lottery ticket. You informed them you possessed the lottery ticket. They sent someone to acquire it from you. That person died in a fiery blast, and XM Investments did not receive their prize. You, Ms. Robertson, are currently living on overtime. We want to extend that overtime by one more year. On the other hand, if the legal representative does appear on behalf of XM Investments to make a claim on the jackpot prize, we can proceed with a criminal investigation. If there is a criminal investigation opened into this matter, we can continue to provide you with protection, so long as you continue to cooperate with our efforts. Do you understand what I am saying to you?"

"Yes," replied Maureen.

"There is one more thing, Ms. Robertson," said Interim Director Ward. "The legal representative you are utilizing to set this canary trap. What is the likelihood of XM Investments executing that person, in accordance with the tying up of loose ends that Attorney General Haynes spoke of?"

"That is not likely to happen at all," replied Maureen. "The person I chose is much too valuable of an asset to XM Investments. He is an international legal guru who possesses the uncanny ability at keeping them off the grid. No, they will not touch him."

⌘⌘⌘

THIRTY-TWO

It was a stormy December day in Savannah, Georgia. The sky was as dark as night at two o'clock in the afternoon, while snow and sleet mercilessly pelted the mansion's grotesquely oversized bay windows.

But for as dark and stormy as the elements were outside, they paled in comparison to the tempest brewing within the walls of this stately Georgian mansion.

Clayton Hicks was on a rampage. He scampered from room to room, shouting obscenities as he drained the contents of every bottle of brandy he came across.

"I am doomed," he said, clutching onto a bottle of brandy, while sliding his back down a wall onto the floor. "There is nowhere I can go to hide from these menacing creatures. They are jackals, and will stop at nothing to get their money."

Clayton raised the bottle of brandy to his mouth. It was empty.

Angered, Clayton tossed the bottle down a long corridor. As it crashed, he muttered, "It serves me right for thinking I could continue to sleep with expensive prostitutes all these years without karma catching up to me."

Earlier that day, Clayton received a visit from a man known to the rich, and powerful, as a "pleasure broker."

The man, who went by the name Cypris, had come to deliver some dire news to Clayton. It was time to pay his tab for services rendered.

Over the years, Clayton had developed a taste for exotic women. Using his esteemed international reputation as collateral, Clayton engaged the world of high-dollar escorts, utilizing Cypris' brokerage services to arrange the trysts.

However, Clayton was only eager to pay for his brandy. For his sexual escapades, Clayton opened credit tabs with those who fed his frenzy.

As a result, Clayton racked upwards of six million dollars in lines of credit with multiple human-trafficking cartels for access to these women. But the cartels were now closing his tabs. It was time to pay in full, and they needed payment now.

                    ☙☙☙

Cypris informed Clayton that the cartels would kill him if payment were not made in full within one week.

Clayton was crushed. He was a poor money manager, and accustomed to living the life of luxury. The monthly retainer he received from XM Investments was indeed handsome, but not enough to cover this tab.

Downtrodden, Clayton staggered towards his bedroom, but stopped when he reached the den. "Hmmm," he grumbled, and then slumbered to his desk.

He retrieved the envelope that had been delivered to him by armed courier several months prior. He then emptied its contents onto his desk.

Clayton glanced over the written instructions that Maureen had provided, and tossed them aside. He then picked up the lottery ticket, and said, "I have no idea how much you are worth. But, if you were worthy of an armed courier delivery service, it might very well be enough to pay my debts."

He then strode to his bedroom to pass out.

                    ☙☙☙

The following morning, Clayton suffered from a massive hangover. However, it was quickly cured after he went online to visit the Iowa lottery website to learn more about this ticket.

"Mary, mother of Joseph," he said, cupping his mouth with his hand. "This darn thing is worth over $16 million! It is no wonder they used an armed courier to deliver this to me. But why has XM not contacted me about my not cashing this in? That is strange indeed. Nevertheless, the timing here is impeccable. According to the Iowa lottery, the last day to make a claim for this prize is in five days."

Clayton rose from his computer, looked at the ticket in his hand and said, "Well, then, if claiming you is what I must do to save myself, then I will do just that. I will set aside my pride, and complete this trivial task to satisfy those greedy cartel jackals. But first, I must quickly prepare the necessary documents to create an emergency Trust under XM's name…"

⌘⌘⌘

THIRTY-THREE

DES MOINES, IOWA
DECEMBER 28, 2011

Iowa Lottery Commissioner Kevin Renalds was on his mobile phone with his wife when his office line rang.

Looking at the caller ID, he saw it was from the reception area. He then said to his wife, "sweetie, listen, I really do not want to go to your parents for New Year's Eve. Can we talk about this when I get home? I have a call to pick up."

Commissioner Renalds ended the call with his wife, and picked up his office phone.

The receptionist shouted, "Holy cow Commissioner Renalds, the ticket is here! The winner!"

Commissioner Renalds replied, "Someone is here with a winning ticket? That is great. I will be down to congratulate them, in a few minutes."

The receptionist excitedly said, "No, not A winner. THE winner! The Hot Ticket that expires tomorrow at midnight! That ticket!"

∾∾∾

Pandemonium struck the Iowa Capitol complex, as phones at the Attorney General's Office, Governor's Office, the Iowa Safety & Intelligence Bureau, and other agencies rang off the hook.

It was not long before the media was notified of an out-of-state attorney who had presented himself to make a jackpot claim on the Hot Ticket worth $16.5 million.

Mystery, and conspiracy theories, had taken a life of their own over the previous year regarding who purchased the winning ticket, and why such a large prize had yet to be claimed.

The local news media continually fanned the flames of conspiracy, riding the waves of local hysteria as the deadline for making a claim approached.

Behind closed doors, and armed with the knowledge obtained from Maureen Robertson, newly appointed Director Ward, Attorney General Haynes, Commissioner Renalds and his top fraud investigator Special Agent Jennings, pressed Clayton Hicks for details regarding the chain of events which led to him making this claim.

"All I can tell you," replied Clayton, "is that the personal identity of my client must remain anonymous. Thus, the funds will be deposited into a Trust created for the benefit of my client."

"What is the name of that Trust?" Commissioner Renalds asked.

"The Trust name is XM Investments," replied Clayton.

Special Agent Jennings asked, "Is that Trust based in Belize?"

"It is," replied Clayton, clearing his throat.

"We need to know more," pressed Director Ward. "Who bought the ticket? How did this ticket get into your hands? How is the person who bought this ticket connected to a Trust in Belize?"

The questions kept coming, but Clayton could not answer. When it became apparent to him that no answer would suffice, he stood up, buttoned his suit jacket, and said, "The laws regulating Iowa's lottery are contradictory to my client's interests. You require full identification. My client requires full anonymity. We are at an impasse, my dear Iowans, and I cannot yield."

Clayton wiped sweat from his forehead. He knew that his next words would solidify his fate at the hands of the cartels. However, if he were to give the Iowa officials what they were asking for, his fate would be much worse at the hands of XM operatives.

"And, so it is," Clayton said lowly to himself.

Clayton then said, "It is because of this impasse that I must withdraw my claim on this jackpot."

"Woah, wait," said Special Agent Jennings. "You are leaving $16.5 million on the table because you do not wish to reveal the identity of who bought this winning ticket?"

"It is not that I do not wish," replied Clayton, as he exited the conference room. "It is that I cannot."

⌘⌘⌘

FINAL CHAPTER

The world breaks everyone, and afterward, some are strong at the broken places. - Ernest Hemingway

Maureen Robertson finished packing her belongings. Sitting at the edge of her bed inside one of the many safe houses she had been placed in over the previous months, she cried.

"This is it," sobbed Maureen. "XM did not make a claim on the lottery ticket winnings. They obviously managed to stop Clayton from coming forward. I was so wrong about his worth to them. He is most likely dead, and it is my fault. They will be coming for me soon. The deadline for claiming the jackpot is tomorrow night, and I will be tossed out like a dog."

She dropped backwards onto the bed for one final good night's sleep, when the door to the house she was in burst open.

"Grab her, now!" Commanded a male voice. "We are going into level four security detail mode. Move it!"

Maureen felt her heart jump into her throat. She feared what could be happening. Was there an attack occurring? There were so many people yelling. What was going on?

The door to Maureen's bedroom flung open. A strong looking woman entered without hesitation, saying, "Ma'am, we need to get you out of here, right now."

Maureen gasped, "But...what? Why?"

The woman did not answer. Instead, she grabbed Maureen, and hustled her out of the house, towards an awaiting SUV.

Several other agents by the SUV stuffed Maureen into the vehicle, then tapped on the roof of the vehicle to let the driver know it was time to drive.

The driver revved the SUV's engine, and tore off into the night.

❧ ❧ ❧

Maureen asked the driver, "Where are we going?"

"I don't know where you're going," the driver replied. "But I am headed to someplace warm, with lots of jungles that are teeming with wildlife salivating at the mere thought of eating a human."

"I'm sorry, what?" Maureen asked in disbelief.

The driver parked the SUV, and turned towards Maureen, with a large grin on his face.

"Augustus, is that really you?" Maureen cried.

"Last I checked, there is no one else as cute as I am, so yeah," Augustus jokingly replied.

"How did you? –"

Augustus cut her off, saying, "We don't have much time, Maureen. They will quickly learn you are not being driven by one of their agents. I wanted to thank you for your bravery, and tenacity. You did it, you know?"

"No. I do not know. What?" Maureen replied.

Augustus said, "Your guy came to claim the lottery jackpot today, and all Hell broke loose. In fact, he made your information even more credible when he decided that too many questions were being asked of him."

"What do you mean?" Maureen asked.

"He withdrew the claim, and left the $16.5 million on the table," answered Augustus.

Augustus saw flashing lights in the distance, and said, "It is time for me to go, my dear. Be sure to tell them it was me who drove you here, and that I wanted to congratulate you."

"Please stay," Maureen pleaded.

"I can't, Maureen," replied Augustus. "I've murdered people in cold blood to get to the truth, to include corrupt federal agents. No matter how justified I was in doing so, I will never be exonerated. I have no choice but to disappear. Besides, I am ill, Maureen, and have a lot of healing to do."

Augustus exited the SUV, waved a kiss to Maureen, and disappeared.

৵৵৵

Augustus stepped out from a cornfield upon seeing a white van pull to the side of the road.

The van's side door slid open, and Augustus entered.

Cardinal Lara looked back to Augustus from the driver seat, and said, "God has allowed you this moment of closure, my dear son. But your illness is rapidly taking you away, and you must complete your spiritual healing before your day comes.

"I understand, Cardinal," replied Augustus.

Cardinal Lara turned, put on the radio, and pulled back onto the roadway. The radio crackled with live local news from Des Moines:

> "Iowa officials today announced a criminal probe into an out-of-state attorney's attempt at claiming the mysterious Hot Ticket lottery jackpot of $16.5 million. Although investigators have not revealed much, they did share with the press that the attorney attempted to claim the ticket on behalf of a Trust named XM Investments, which is based in the Central American country of Belize…"

> "In other news, Senate Intelligence Committee chairman Clyde Williams has called an emergency session of Congress, and has subpoenaed NSA officials to testify before the committee. Anonymous sources have confirmed that Prentiss Gates, and Saxby Coles are the first of several intelligence community officials to appear before the committee due to their involvement in what the Pentagon refers to as crimson operations."

> "Elsewhere in the Capitol, DC police this morning reported the suicide death of Frank Newberry, who served as the Director for Internal Matters at the NSA…"

Augustus smiled, and said to Cardinal Lara, "I am now fully prepared to go."

C C C

About the Author

O. Nicholas Cicero is a native New Yorker, born and raised in the borough of Brooklyn. He currently resides in the Midwest, and passed the bar examinations of Iowa, and Minnesota. He received his Bachelor of Arts degree from The University of Iowa, and Juris Doctorate from The University of Tulsa College of Law. Post law school, the author worked for federal, and state regulatory agencies in various capacities.

SEE BOOK ONE OF THE AUGUSTUS PEÑA SERIES

www.ingramcontent.com/pod-product-compliance
Lightning Source LLC
Chambersburg PA
CBHW072110170626
46813CB00004B/1495